Wish We Were There

There

Lionel Hart

CONTENTS

Chapter One
Parker

THEN

Pop-punk Sensation *Get Well Soon* Frontman Zach Ross Dead at 29, Others Injured, in Tour Bus Crash

Punk News Net, August 4

by Parker Flores

Zach Ross, lead singer of Get Well Soon, was reported dead this evening following a collision involving their tour bus and an unidentified driver. He was 29 years old.

The members of Get Well Soon, their bus driver, and the driver of the other vehicle were all taken to the hospital, where Ross was pronounced deceased. No further information about the other driver is available at this time, but witnesses report the unidentified driver was behaving erratically and initially attempted to leave the scene.

Get Well Soon has canceled all upcoming tour dates, which were scheduled to run for another three weeks, in light of the accident. Keyboardist Taylor Lewis-Ross and guitarist Angie Gomez were also injured in the crash, but are expected to be discharged from the hospital shortly.

Punk News Net has followed the career of Ross and Get Well Soon for several years, and we're devastated to hear about this. Zach, Taylor, Angie, Dean, and Kylie are personal friends to much of the PNN staff, and we extend our sincerest condolences to them, especially Zach's husband Taylor and all his family and friends.

More information will be added as it becomes available.

Updated August 5

Taylor Lewis-Ross and Angie Gomez were both discharged from the hospital this morning. They have declined to comment at this time.

The driver of the other vehicle was allegedly arrested for driving under the influence after being discharged from the hospital.

No crowdfunding or other donations have been established by members of the band at this time. The members of Get Well Soon kindly ask that any donations fans wish to send are given to a local LGBTQ charity of their choice.

//

Now

"Whenever you're ready."

Parker leaned back in his chair, watching Taylor sitting across from him. Between them, his recording gear was set up on the table: his laptop and a microphone in front of him, and a second mic in front of Taylor. The other man nodded in acknowledgment, but took a long moment before glancing back up at Parker. His dirty blond hair fell into his face as he glanced down at his lap; his right arm was still in a cast, three months after everything.

Finally, Taylor turned his gaze up, blue eyes meeting Parker's. "Ready," he said softly. Parker's heart squeezed at the determined expression on his face.

"Hey, everyone, it's Parker here again with another episode of The Indie Advocate," he began, the rehearsed words coming easily. "This is episode one hundred and eighteen, and our guest today is none other than the incredibly talented Taylor Lewis-Ross, keyboardist for pop-punk powerhouse Get Well Soon."

"Hello, everyone," Taylor said, leaning closer to the mic with a shaky smile on his face.

"As you know, there was unfortunately a terrible accident a few months ago involving Get Well Soon, where the tour bus was hit by a drunk driver," Parker continued. "And sadly, the lead singer and Taylor's husband Zach passed away in the crash. Get Well Soon has been on hiatus since then, and hasn't really released any statements, so—"

"Right, this is the first time we're saying anything publicly," Taylor added. Parker nodded and gestured for him to continue. "And I just want to make it clear from the beginning, this whole thing was my idea. No one on our team is asking me to do this, and Parker didn't ask me. I pitched this to him. I loved his podcast and figured, well, since I'm ready to talk about things, this would be the best place to do so."

Parker smiled. His heart ached in his chest—half in relief and thankfulness for Taylor's transparency, and half in grief that they were having this conversation at all. "That's right. And, in the interest of full disclosure, Taylor and I have actually been friends for, what, ten years now?"

"We went to college together," Taylor added, managing a small smile as he met Parker's gaze. "Parker was actually the one who introduced me to Zach. He even gave a speech at our wedding. I don't think Get Well Soon would have become a thing if it weren't for him. Have you ever told that story on the podcast?"

Parker laughed, shaking his head as he winced. "I sure haven't. But that's okay. We're here to talk about you, and Zach, and the future of Get Well Soon. And anything else you want to talk about while you're here. Usually these interviews are a little more structured, but this isn't really like any other situation I've covered before, so I'm letting you take the reins here. Do you want to tell that story?"

"Sure," Taylor agreed, nodding. Parker held back a sigh of relief—even thinking about it made him emotional still—as the other man continued, "Well, Parker and I became friends because we were in a few classes together. I think it was a poetry class, right?"

"Yeah, poetry," Parker agreed, chuckling.

"I was a music major, and Parker was in journalism. I was interested in writing songs even then, so I took the poetry credit," Taylor said. "And Parker was friends with Zach, who was wanting to put a band together."

"Zach lived in the same dorm as me our freshman year," Parker added. "And I can confirm he was just as charismatic then. Everyone he met was his friend. Everybody loved him."

Taylor's eyes softened as he nodded. "I think it was love at first sight for me. Parker introduced us, we played a few songs together, and the rest is history."

"A lot of history there," Parker murmured. Taylor nodded, and Parker continued, "But we've still been friends since then. Although, once Get Well Soon started really blowing up, we didn't see each other nearly as much, understandably. Zach was charismatic, but he was also an amazing singer and was super dedicated to the band and its success. What was that like for you? Did you think from the beginning that the band you guys had together would make it this far?"

Taylor laughed. "You know, I didn't really think so... But Zach? He always believed one hundred percent that the band was gonna make it big. When we were younger, a lot of people thought he was too idealistic and didn't understand what the real world was like, but I think he always knew. He just knew that he was dedicated enough to make it happen. And when he decided he was in something for the long haul, that was it—yeah, he knew right away."

"Like with you," Parker said, and Taylor's fond smile faltered.

"Yeah," he replied. "Like with us. I think a lot of people thought that would be another thing that would keep the band from being successful—that Zach wanted to make

this kind of music as an openly gay man, and openly
married too. I think a lot of people would expect him to
either play up the hot, single gay guy kind of persona, or be
totally closeted until he became successful; but Zach was
always super authentic, no matter where he was or what he
was doing. He wanted to be the next, you know, My Chem,
or Fall Out Boy, or whatever, and he knew he wanted to be
completely out as himself. He didn't see it as two separate
things he had to choose between."

"I mean, it took a long time to see that kind of success,
didn't it?" Parker asked. "Did he have that conviction the
entire time? Get Well Soon has been a band for almost a
decade, but it's only been the past two or three years that
you guys really blew up."

Taylor nodded. "Honestly, I really think he believed it
would happen the whole time. That's what kept him going,
even when we were only making money by touring and
barely breaking even. I tried to talk to him about me getting
a part-time job separate from the band a bunch of times,
but he never wanted me to make the jump. But it also
meant he was ready to keep hustling when things finally
started looking up. So when Wish We Were There blew
up on TikTok, he understood how to keep the momentum
going. And here we are. Big sold-out summer tour in all

these stadiums and bigger venues than we've ever played in..."

He trailed off with a sigh. "So much for that, I guess."

"You were about halfway through the summer tour when the accident happened," Parker said softly. "How much of that day do you remember?"

"I remember all of it," Taylor said, his voice taking on a cooler tone, as if he were steeling himself to face what came next. "I was still awake when the bus crashed. I was in my bunk, and Zach and Angie were sitting up front chatting with Bobby, our driver, and..."

He trailed off, looking down at the mic silently for a long moment. Parker winced—Taylor had seemed so sure he'd wanted to do this, but from the start, Parker had only been worried about him. It had been three months, but wasn't that still too soon? It didn't seem so long ago. He couldn't imagine being ready to talk about something like this after just three months, but Taylor had been insistent. Now, though, he looked just as uncertain as Parker felt.

"Take your time," Parker said softly. Taylor blinked, giving a slight start as if he'd forgotten Parker was there entirely, then he nodded.

"The bus fell onto its side, which is how I got knocked out of my bunk and broke my wrist," he said, holding up his arm, still in a cast. "Angie broke her foot, but our driver

Bobby and Dean and Kylie only got a little scraped up. And Zach..."

Taylor sucked in a shuddering breath, looking away.

"Zach, he... *Fuck*," he hissed, rubbing his face with his one good hand. "Sorry, can we take a break?"

"Yeah, yeah," Parker agreed quickly, reaching for his laptop to pause the recording. "Do you need anything? Can I help?"

"I just—I need a minute," Taylor replied as he stood up abruptly. Without saying anything else, he hurried out of the room, leaving Parker in his office.

He sat there alone for a moment, mind racing. Taylor was his friend, but he had no idea what he was supposed to do or how to help. His husband was dead, and Parker knew that if he had been in Taylor's place, there was nothing anyone could say to him that might make him feel even remotely better.

It didn't help that his heart still skipped a beat every time he looked at Taylor. A decade ago, it had been his biggest regret in life that he hadn't asked Taylor out before introducing him to Zach. He'd long ago made his peace with it, but the crush he'd had from the first time they'd met had never fully gone away. Parker had never said anything, and he never would, but it only made the situation feel even more fucked up than it already was.

Parker stared at the far wall of his studio for a long moment, eyes scanning the myriad tour posters and mounted album covers. Should he try to comfort Taylor? Or would it be better to leave him alone and give him space?

Finally, Parker sighed and stepped out of his office. His apartment was comfortable but far from spacious, so he found Taylor again quickly; the other man had gone out onto the balcony, his back turned to Parker in the living room. Parker watched him for a moment, still unsure of what to do, as Taylor stood motionless staring out at the San Diego skyline.

He pulled himself together, grabbed two cans of sparkling water from his fridge, and opened the glass door to the balcony. Taylor turned to face him, his eyes red-rimmed, but a faint, resolute smile on his features.

"Sorry," Taylor repeated. "I really thought I could do this, but... I don't know."

"Don't apologize," Parker interjected, handing him the sparkling water. Taylor took it without question. "We can skip it. Or we can take a break if you want. It's your call."

Taylor didn't respond right away, looking down pensively at the beverage he held.

"Hey," Parker said softly. Before he could think better of it, he reached out to grab Taylor's hand. His hand hovered uncertainly above Taylor's wrist for just a moment, then he gently placed his palm on Taylor's forearm, the hard material of his cast cool and scratchy against Parker's open palm. Taylor didn't pull away. His blue eyes flickered up to meet Parker's concerned gaze, then back down to where Parker was touching him. "We'll take things at your pace, okay? It's alright if you don't want to do this after all. I have other interviews saved I could do for this episode instead. Everyone would understand if you decide you aren't ready to talk about it yet."

Somehow, Taylor's expression only became more pained, but after a beat, he managed a watery smile in response.

"I really wanted to talk about it, you know?" he finally said, his voice coming out scratchy. "It really felt like I was ready. Like I might explode without being able to talk about it. But now... I don't know. Actually talking about it feels so different from thinking about talking about it. About him. And the band, and everything... It all just fucking sucks, you know?"

Despite himself, Parker stifled a bark of a laugh. Taylor let out a small chuckle, too.

"Yeah," Parker agreed. "It really sucks."

Taylor set down his drink on the railing of the balcony, then placed his hand on top of Parker's, where it still rested on the cast. Parker's heartbeat quickened in response, and he was sure Taylor could feel the thrum of his rapid pulse where their skin touched.

God, what was wrong with him? Taylor was his friend, coming to him for comfort after his husband fucking died, and he was still reacting like the lovesick boy he'd been all those years ago.

But Taylor squeezed his hand gratefully, his palm warm against Parker's fingers. "Thank you," Taylor said, his voice trembling. "For understanding. And being here for me. I really... I really appreciate it."

The words wouldn't come, so Parker only nodded and gave the other man's forearm a light squeeze. After a moment, Taylor pulled his hand away.

"We can just cancel today," he offered, opening the untouched sparkling water that was still in his hand.

"Let's reschedule," Taylor replied, his voice sounding firmer now. "I still want to do this. Really, Parker, I do. I just... need to think. I need to figure out what I want to say. Are you free tomorrow?"

"Okay," Parker agreed, pulling his phone from his pocket. "Are you sure you want to do it tomorrow? It isn't too soon?"

"Tomorrow," Taylor repeated, and Parker chuckled.

"Yeah, I can do the same time tomorrow," he said after glancing over his schedule. He'd planned to spend tomorrow working on the one article a week he was still writing for Punk News Net, but he could do that today instead of editing the podcast recording. If he could get the article busted out today, Tim wouldn't give him any shit for his podcast again.

"Thank you," Taylor said, smiling shakily at him again. "I... I think I'm just gonna go home. Figure out what it is I want to say. Maybe make some notes or something, I don't know."

Parker grinned. "Yeah, sounds good. Whatever you wanna do."

Suddenly Taylor was beside him, squeezing him in a hug with his good arm. Parker's heart had only just slowed back down to a normal rate, but skyrocketed all over again at the unexpected contact. He returned the hug slowly—was it grief or longing that made his throat feel so tight?

Taylor held him for a long moment, far longer than Parker would have expected. But he couldn't let himself think too much about it—Taylor was his friend. He just went through a traumatic experience. Of course he would need affection and care. That was all.

"Thank you," Taylor said softly, before stepping away. "I really appreciate it, Parker. You're seriously the best."

"I—Well, yeah, no problem," Parker stammered, still unsure of how to react.

"I should go," Taylor said, slipping past Parker back into his apartment. "I'll see you tomorrow, okay?"

"Yeah, okay," Parker said faintly, watching him leave.

He realized just as Taylor was slipping out the front door that his drink was still on the railing, forgotten. "I—yeah, tomorrow. Okay."

Chapter Two
Taylor

Taylor was out of Parker's apartment and halfway through the elevator ride back down to the first floor before his face finally stopped burning. What the hell was wrong with him? What was he even doing?

For months, all he could focus on was how badly he wanted to talk about Zach, how much he wanted to *tell Parker* about everything; but now here he was, running away from his first opportunity. He'd wanted this—he really, truly had. And then he was in front of Parker with his warm eyes and his friendly smile, and all the words he'd rehearsed in his head were completely gone. Zach would have been disappointed in him.

As the elevator dinged, and the door slid open, Taylor stifled a groan and rubbed his face with his good hand. And hugging Parker like that, too? The last time he had hugged Parker was at Zach's funeral. There hadn't been anything weird about it then, but *that* was definitely weird. What the hell would Parker think of him now?

No, Parker was sweet. He was kind and understanding, and he knew Taylor better than just about anyone. He wouldn't think anything of it. It was a hug between friends, nothing out of the ordinary. Taylor was the one being weird about it. Hopefully, Parker hadn't picked up on it.

He kept ruminating on it for the entire drive home, wondering what possessed him to do it, and alternating between immense regret and the thought of hugging him again tomorrow. He was touch-starved, he decided when he was turning at the light onto his street, and that was it.

Another car was parked in front of his house, making his heart leap into his throat. It took him a moment to recognize it as Kylie's car. What the hell was she doing here?

Her car door opened, and she scrambled to get out as he pulled into the driveway. His chest ached with guilt. Maybe he had been avoiding everyone too much if she was showing up at his house.

"Taylor!" she called. Her hair was a bright acid green today—it had been yellow the day of the crash and at Zach's funeral, but he wasn't sure if he had seen her at all since then. "What the hell, dude? I've been trying to get ahold of you for days!"

For one wild moment, Taylor considered hurrying inside and locking the door behind him. It wasn't that he didn't want to see Kylie, not really—everyone in the band was friends—but the prospect of facing her, or any of his bandmates, made him feel sick to his stomach.

But Kylie had clearly been worried about him if she'd been waiting for him to come home. So he gritted his teeth and stood there as she hurried up the driveway to join him at the front door. Her outfit looked perfectly put together—a crop top under an oversized, dark jacket, black and white plaid pants, and black combat boots—which only made him feel sloppy and unkempt in comparison. His style had always been more plain compared to Kylie's and Zach's, but seeing how perfectly normal she looked made him even more self-conscious. He'd just thrown on a t-shirt and jeans and his Converse—all casually grunge at best—but his shirt was wrinkled, and his hair was messy.

He hadn't felt it with Parker, but looking at Kylie made him feel painfully aware that the rest of the world had gone on without him.

"Hi," he managed to croak out. "Uh... sorry."

Kylie scoffed, but despite her scowl, she pulled him into a tight hug.

"You can't just disappear like that, dude," she grumbled. "We're all worried about you."

"Sorry," he repeated, unsure of what else to say. "Come on, let's go inside at least."

His and Zach's house had always been like a second home to the other members of the band, so it was jarring to see Kylie moving with such uncertainty as she followed him in, like a scared animal in an unfamiliar place. She stood awkwardly in the middle of the living room before she sat down gingerly on the armchair across from the couch, where Taylor flopped down miserably.

"Get on with it, then," he sighed, gesturing for her to continue, which only made her frown deepen.

"What, you think I'm here to yell at you?" she replied, then winced. "Wait, that came out sounding like yelling. Taylor, I'm not here because I'm mad at you, alright? I was just worried. We all are. No one's heard from you in weeks. I just wanted to make sure you were okay."

"I'm not okay," he said dryly.

"You know what I meant," she huffed. "Taylor, I'm sorry. I just wanted to check up on you."

All his irritation deflated at that, and he sighed. "I know. You're right. I'm sorry too."

Kylie's expression immediately softened. "I just wish you would have said something if you needed some time to yourself. It made us really worried to have you drop off the face of the Earth out of nowhere. We were really freaked out because you seemed like you were doing okay, and then there was just... nothing."

"I understand," Taylor said. "I didn't mean to ignore you, really. I just... I don't know. I guess I just didn't want to talk." He almost added that he didn't want to talk *to anyone*, but that wasn't entirely true.

"Where were you just now?" Kylie asked.

"Parker's apartment," he said flatly, then added before she could make a comment, "I wanted to be on his podcast. That's it."

He refused to look at her, but he could easily imagine all the different ways she might react. When he finally risked the glance, though, her expression was purposely, carefully blank.

"His podcast, huh?" she said lightly. "What did you talk about?"

"Just... Zach and the band," Taylor replied. Silence hung between them for a long moment. He knew what she wanted to ask, and it was the last thing he wanted to answer.

There was more he needed to say, too, more that he'd been avoiding.

"Listen, I need to tell you," he blurted out. His stomach did a flip-flop—there was no taking it back now. "That I, uh... I decided I'm done with the band."

Kylie stared at him for a long moment, brows furrowed, eyes wide. He was sweating with nerves—under his cast, his right arm started to itch terribly. But he held her gaze for as long as he could, until finally she asked in a carefully calm tone,

"Have you told this to anyone else? Is that what you were talking about with Parker?"

He swallowed hard. "No. You're the first person I've told."

She stared at him silently for a moment longer, then leaned back in the armchair with a long, drawn-out sigh.

"I... I don't know what to say, Taylor," she said faintly, reaching up to run an anxious hand through her long green hair. "I mean... Like, I get it, and I can't really be mad, but I *want* to be mad about it. Fuck, dude. Are you serious?"

"Yeah," Taylor replied, looking down at his good hand clasped hard around the cast.

"But you said you weren't gonna leave," she protested, an edge of despair in her voice that made Taylor squeeze his eyes shut.

"I changed my mind," he croaked, shaking his head. "I can't do it, Kylie. And, honestly, I don't think we should. It's never gonna be the same without Zach. He was the entire face of the band. Without him..."

"Tom left Blink and they're fine," she protested, and despite himself, Taylor laughed aloud.

"Yeah, they are," he said. "But as much as I hate to say it, Kylie, we aren't exactly Blink-182, so, you know. And, plus, he came back."

Kylie laughed bitterly at that, shaking her head. "Speak for yourself, dude. Man, fuck you, seriously."

"I know," he murmured, managing a slight smile. Despite her words, her tone was lighter than he would have expected. "That's kind of why I've been avoiding everyone. I was still thinking about it, then when I decided, I was... dreading telling you guys."

"Yeah, Dean and Angie aren't gonna be happy," Kylie sighed, leaning forward to prop her head in her hand. She looked at Taylor for a long moment, lips pursed in thought. He didn't know how to respond, so he just waited, wondering how badly he'd just imploded all her plans for the future.

Get Well Soon had been on the up. Maybe they would have been more like Blink-182 in another year—Zach sure believed so. Would he be pissed that Taylor was throwing in the towel so easily? Would he have understood?

Did it even matter? Zach was gone.

"So what are you going to do, then?" Kylie finally asked him, pulling him from his thoughts.

"What do you mean?" he asked.

"I mean, are you gonna start your own band now?" she pressed. "Capitalism and everything. Gotta do something, you know?"

He bit back a laugh. He hadn't told anyone about his plans either—he'd considered telling Parker, but when he'd choked up about Zach, it had left his mind entirely. But if Kylie was the first to know, that was good, too. Out of all his bandmates, he and Kylie were the closest; not that he wasn't friends with Angie or Dean, but something about him and Kylie had just clicked early on. Kylie always said that it was because he was a Libra and she was a Taurus. He wasn't sure how much stock he put into that sort of thing; but it made sense in a way, dreamy air signs and grounded earth signs balancing out.

But her groundedness made him nervous about telling her his plan, too. She'd find out eventually, though, so he might as well be the first to tell her.

"I think I'm done making music entirely," he said quickly, before he could overthink it more than he already had. "Instead, I want to... I want to set up a music venue. A queer-focused venue."

Her brows furrowed in consternation, but she didn't respond right away. He added nervously,

"I already have a place in mind. Zed Miller is selling The Bridge, so I think I'm going to buy it off him and renovate it."

"Renovate it?!" she blurted out, as if that was the most unbelievable part of what he'd just revealed. "Taylor, have you ever done a reno in your life?"

"No," he said self-consciously. "But, I mean, I talked to him about it, and it didn't seem that bad—just replacing parts of the stage and repainting and stuff."

She shot a pointed look at his arm in the cast. Embarrassed, he shifted the way he sat, so it was more behind him.

"How are you going to renovate it with one arm?" she said, and he shrugged.

"I don't know," he said. "I haven't even bought the damn venue yet, Kylie, so sorry I don't have all the details figured out. I have the money for it. I'll figure it out. But I want to do this."

"You're gonna open a music venue," she repeated faintly. He nodded, willing the heat to fade from his cheeks. Once her initial shock subsided, he knew that she'd be excited and curious. "Well, shit. I guess that's pretty cool. You *really* don't think you'll want to be in a band, though?"

He sighed, scrubbing his good hand through his hair. He really needed to shower. What the hell had he been thinking, showing up to Parker's so scruffy like this?

"I don't know," he said softly, the words feeling more confessional than anything else that he'd said so far. "It won't be the same. So much of it was just... *Zach.* I wrote some songs, but he made them *good.* And with my wrist..."

He trailed off. That felt too personal to say, even to Kylie. The doctors had told him he would definitely play piano again, but some part of him was completely convinced his musical ability would be entirely gone when the cast came off. He'd already gone so long without practicing, without so much as touching his keyboard, after playing it every day for almost his entire life.

"It hasn't healed yet?" Kylie asked softly, brows furrowed in concern.

"It's not that," he said hurriedly, trying to move on. "I just... I guess maybe someday I could try again. But right now, I just really don't ever want to write another song."

Kylie's expression crumpled at that. "Aw, babes. That's really sad."

He shrugged. "It's fine. It was mostly Zach anyway."

She let out a long, slow sigh, mulling everything over. "He really messed everything up, didn't he? Going and dying like that."

Taylor stifled a laugh. It was a strange relief to know that they could joke about it now.

"Super inconsiderate of him," he murmured, and Kylie chuckled.

"Should I tell Dean and Angie?" she asked, her voice more serious now. Part of Taylor wanted her to be the one to break the news, just so he didn't have to do it, so the offer was tempting. But if he was going to be the one to pull the plug, they deserved to hear it from him.

"No," he forced himself to say. "No, I should tell them."

"I think that would be best, too," she agreed. "Don't wait too long, though, okay? They're worried about you, too. And the band being in limbo like this is stressful for everyone."

He nodded grimly. "I will."

They remained in silence for a beat, then Kylie stifled a giggle behind her hand.

"So you were with Parker, huh?" she teased, and he rolled his eyes, hoping the flush creeping up his face wasn't obvious.

"I told you it was for his podcast," he said. "And I talked for like ten minutes before I freaked out and bailed. So I'm seeing him again tomorrow to hopefully record something decent for him. That's it."

Her expression softened as he spoke. "Well, I'm glad you're talking to him, at least, if you're not talking to us."

"I'm not *not* talking to you," Taylor protested, but she laughed and waved him away, standing up.

"Yeah, yeah," she said. "I just came to check on you, so I'll get out of your hair. Answer my texts every once in a while now, okay? Let's plan something with Dean and Angie soon."

He watched her go pensively. "Yeah, soon."

Chapter Three
Parker

THEN

"Hey, you, uh, you said you play piano, right?"

Parker remembered that Taylor played piano, of course, but he wasn't sure how else to bring it up; and the sight of the cutest guy in his poetry class still made his heart beat faster and his brain not work correctly. The other boy blinked up owlishly at him from where he'd taken his seat next to Parker. His big blue eyes widened at first—the way they always did when Parker started talking to him, as if surprised all over again at his attention—then they crinkled with a smile as Taylor nodded.

"Yeah, I do," he replied, his voice lilting with a stifled laugh—they had talked about their majors before, of course, so he *knew* Parker knew he played piano. "Why?"

"I have a friend who's starting a band," Parker continued, sitting down next to him. "And he's looking for a keyboardist. Think you might be interested in something like that?"

Taylor hesitated. "Oh, uh... Well, maybe. What kind of music?"

Asking him seemed like a mistake, Parker thought. Taylor was so *pretty*, with his dirty blonde hair falling elegantly to his shoulders and the sweet pink flush to his skin, the way his eyes brightened when he smiled—he looked like he should be an art student sculpting masterpieces, or painting lovely ethereal landscapes, not at all like a member of a rock band like Zach was envisioning. But when Zach said he'd been looking for a keyboardist, Parker had mentioned the cute guy in his poetry class who was a music major and played piano; and Zach had all but begged him to put in a good word for him. So here he was, trying to pitch a band that didn't even exist yet to a guy who was probably more suited to playing Beethoven and Bach.

"Er," Parker said. They had been staring at each other in silence for several awkward seconds. "Do you know My Chemical Romance?"

Taylor's expression morphed into one of surprise, then amusement, as he snorted with laughter. "Yeah, I know them."

"That kind of music. Sort of," Parker laughed. "That would be the closest band I can think of that has a keyboardist that I thought you'd know."

Taylor only laughed, covering his mouth with one long-fingered hand, filling Parker with a weird embarrassment, even as his chest ached with longing.

"No worries if you're not into it," he stammered quickly. "He's just looking for a keyboardist, and you play piano, so... I don't know. I told him I'd help him look, so, you know."

"No, I'm—I'm interested," Taylor chuckled before he could yammer on any longer. "It's funny you say that. I've been wanting to try to, uh, expand my repertoire, I guess. So something different like that could be fun. Are there try-outs or something?"

"I don't think he's that organized, no," Parker laughed, half-relieved that Taylor didn't think the question was stupid, but the other half of him now anxious that he would have to follow through with Zach. "I'll text him to let him know you're interested and get more details for you, alright?"

Their professor walked into the room before Taylor could respond, but he whispered over his shoulder as he turned to face the front of the classroom, "Let me know what he says."

Parker nodded, feeling heat rising in his face. If Taylor joined Zach's band, they'd be seeing each other a lot more often. He could find some excuses to hang around their band practices more often, surely, and then maybe...

But he might not even join the band. Parker shook the thoughts away as the professor started on his lecture, trying to focus. Each time he glanced over at Taylor, though, the other boy had a small smile on his face, as if he was thinking the same as Parker.

11

Now

Somehow, Parker managed not to dwell too much on Taylor for the rest of the day. But the other man showed up at his apartment the next morning bright-eyed and put together, and Parker couldn't take his eyes off him. He'd been a little scruffy the day before, sure, but Parker could hardly hold that against him, all things considered. Today, though, he was clean-shaven and his shoulder-length hair was shiny and smooth. He wore an orange flannel with the sleeves half rolled-up over a black t-shirt and skinny jeans with black Converse, looking like he'd walked right out of one of their early album covers.

Something in him had changed in the twenty-four hours they'd been apart—Parker didn't know what, but it was clearly something positive.

He'd been staring at Taylor on his doorstep in silence for way too long. With an unintelligible stammer, he opened the door wider and stepped aside.

"Sorry," he laughed, scrubbing a hand through his short dark hair self-consciously. "Sorry, I—you look good today. Not saying you didn't look good before. Shit. I just..."

Taylor laughed, a faint blush rising in his face as he stepped inside—that, surely, Parker was only imagining.

"No worries," Taylor replied, shaking his head. "I, uh... I really needed to shower. Sorry about yesterday. I didn't realize I looked like such a hot mess until I got home."

"Don't apologize," Parker said quickly. "Seriously. I understand. Do you want anything to eat or drink before we start?"

Taylor grinned and held up a travel mug in his good hand. "No, I'm set."

Parker smiled weakly. "Then let's get started."

They shuffled into his office-turned-recording-studio, which was just the second bedroom in his apartment. Parker sat down in his chair and made sure everything was set to record; Taylor took up the same spot on the small sofa across from him.

"Alright, we're good," he said, nervously glancing up at Taylor. He *really* needed to get over this stupid crush before he made himself look like even more of an idiot. "Ready whenever you are. And like I said yesterday, I'll let you take the lead. Whatever you wanna talk about. Okay?"

"Okay," Taylor said with a nod. He gave Parker a small smile, one that reached his blue eyes today. "I'm ready."

"Let's just pick up where we left off," Parker said. "I'll edit it together, so it should be fine. Test, test... And we're recording."

"You were asking me about the tour, I think," Taylor said. "And... how everything happened."

"Right," Parker replied, gesturing for Taylor to continue.

"I know the autopsy was reported on, so everyone probably already knows," Taylor said, eyes flickering down to the mic on the table in front of him. "God, it was so... *stupid,* you know? He barely got scratched up at all. But when the bus fell over, he just... Hit his head at the exact right angle for it to..."

He trailed off, shaking his head.

"It was just terrible luck," Parker offered softly, and Taylor nodded.

"It just made me realize how fragile everything is," he said. "How easily everything changes. One guy decided to drive drunk, and now... Here we are."

"I know a lot of people are wondering about the other driver," Parker said, and Taylor shook his head.

"I don't want to talk about him," he said quickly, frowning. "It's done. You can't change the past. He's in jail. He's probably going to stay there for a long time. I hate that people even know his name."

"Yeah, that's understandable," Parker replied. "If it wasn't for this one terrible thing he did, no one would have any idea who he is. Why give him the attention?"

"Other than to tell people to not fucking drink and drive," Taylor added. "It's really wild to think about how one other person's decision has completely changed the trajectory of my life, the life of everyone in the band. Zach was achieving his dream, and now the band is..."

He trailed off, looking pained. Parker hesitated, unsure of how much to push—Taylor was his friend, but this was an interview, still. He prided himself on his job as a journalist, but couldn't bring himself to ask his friend anything too hard-hitting.

"I'm sure the fans are wondering about the band, too," he said in as gentle a tone as he could manage. "There haven't really been any announcements, and all the socials have been quiet. I think that's one drawback of being indie in your situation. There's no management team that could handle some of this messaging for you, instead of the band having to worry about it yourselves. Can you share anything about the band, and what you guys are thinking of doing now?"

Taylor paused for a long moment, then finally shook his head. "Nothing has been discussed, really. I think everyone is still just reeling and sorting out how they feel about it all. To be honest, I haven't really talked to them about the future much. I guess I'm... Well, I don't know."

Parker waited. Taylor stared down at the mic in front of him, his expression frozen; clearly he was considering something, but Parker didn't know what. This time, he didn't press.

"Anyway," Taylor continued, glancing away again. Whatever he'd been thinking of saying, he must have decided against it. "I think I was in shock after the accident, to be honest. It didn't really hit me until I realized I would have to... to plan a funeral for him. And all the paperwork. I had no idea there was so much paperwork when someone dies. Insurance, bank stuff, our house... They really don't make it easy. So that sucked. But I think I'm doing alright now... All things considered." He held up his arm in the cast

WISH WE WERE THERE

with a wry smile. "Aside from this. My arm, I mean. Guess that doesn't translate well over audio."

"When are you getting the cast off?" Parker asked, and Taylor winced, putting his arm down.

"I, uh... Missed the appointment to have it taken off and I just haven't rescheduled," he admitted, looking uncomfortable. "The doctor said it was healed by now, but... I don't know. It still hurts sometimes, so I'm nervous to have the cast off. Figure some extra time couldn't hurt, right?"

"I mean, I'm no doctor, but sure," Parker replied, laughing nervously. After a beat, Taylor chuckled, too, sounding much less uncomfortable. "Well, I'm glad to hear you're doing alright. I know you said that there's no update about the future of the band just yet, but Get Well Soon is one of my favorites, so I'd like to talk about the band a little more if that's alright."

Taylor's expression softened. "Yeah, for sure."

//

They ended up talking for another hour, mostly about the band's history and their favorite songs. Zach only came up a few more times; overall, Parker thought it was a good balance for the episode, shedding some light on what happened without lingering too long on the most depressing parts. Once he turned the mics off, though, Taylor shot him an inscrutable look, making him pause with uncertainty.

"Can I... tell you something?" Taylor asked softly, sounding worried all over again. "Off the record?"

"Yeah, of course," Parker answered, even before he'd fully processed what Taylor said. Not that it was an unusual request—he and his podcast guests would often chat about things that weren't public information before or after the recording—but for Taylor to ask in such a way made him unsettled. Taylor let out a long breath, shifting nervously on the couch, which only made Parker more worried.

"It isn't official yet," Taylor finally blurted out. "But... There's probably not going to be a band anymore after all this. I'm leaving Get Well Soon."

Parker blinked. The band would never be the same without Zach, of course, but to hear Taylor confirm it... He couldn't make sense of the jumble of feelings that swelled in his chest. What would happen to the other band members? What would happen to Taylor?

"Oh," he finally managed to croak out. "Are you guys, uh, gonna start a new band, or...?"

Taylor shook his head, but somehow Parker wasn't surprised. "No. Not me, at least. I actually... I've only told Kylie so far."

This must have been what he stopped himself from saying before. He hadn't been talking to the rest of the band because he didn't want to break the bad news.

"That's... I mean, that's a bummer, but you gotta do what you gotta do," Parker said. "It's understandable... after everything. Do you know what you're gonna do once it's official?"

To his surprise, Taylor smiled wryly at him.

"I have an idea, but this is super off the record too," he said. "I'm actually planning on opening a music venue downtown. I already have a space in mind. I wanted something catering to queer indie artists, so... There aren't really any venues like that, so I figured I might as well make one."

Parker's open mouth morphed into a grin. "Taylor, that's awesome. That sounds amazing! Where is it?"

"I haven't signed anything, but Zed Miller is selling The Bridge," Taylor replied. Parker's grin widened. The Bridge had been a popular venue around the time Get Well Soon had first started, and many of their first shows had been there. He remembered it well—he'd covered it countless times, especially in college when he was writing for the school newspaper. It had been mostly local bands at the time, but occasionally larger acts came through. Get Well Soon had still played there once or twice after they got bigger, hosting smaller hometown shows. The venue had been closed for a year or so, but Parker didn't know why.

"I heard it closed down, so that's awesome that you're gonna get it," Parker said, laughing. "I mean, I know you said it's not official, but—c'mon. That's too perfect."

Taylor chuckled. "Yeah, when I heard he was selling it, I thought so, too. It's not official-official yet, but I think it's gonna happen. Will you help me promote it and stuff when it does?"

Parker paused, surprised, then grinned. "Yeah, of course. I'd love to. In fact, you might have already thought of this, but maybe you could do a farewell charity show to kick it off. It'd get a lot of publicity that way, if it's a venue you're opening and Get Well Soon performs its last show there."

The idea seemed perfect to him, but Taylor visibly balked at the suggestion. "I... I don't know. A farewell show would make sense, I guess, but..."

"People love charity shows," Parker protested. "The fans will want to make sure everyone is taken care of."

"I don't need donations for that," Taylor said, shaking his head. "That would seem too cash-grabby, I think."

"Then a charity show for someone else," he offered. "One of the LGBTQ charities you've worked with before, or something like MADD, you know? Something relevant that people will feel a part of."

Taylor was silent for a long moment, making Parker's heart sink. Maybe it wasn't a good idea after all.

"I'll think about it," Taylor finally said, scrubbing a hand through his hair. Parker's disappointment must have been obvious on his face, though, as Taylor added quickly, "It's not that I don't like the idea, Parker, I just... I feel weird thinking about performing at all right now. But it's in the future. It's not even a sure thing."

"Yeah, of course," Parker agreed. "No pressure. Just an idea."

"I'm going to check out the venue next week," Taylor continued brusquely, clearly eager to move on. "Will you come with me? I feel like I'm going to need some moral support."

Again, Parker was taken aback, and he took a moment to process the request before answering.

"You're sure?" he asked. "You don't want Kylie or anyone from the band to go with you?"

Taylor shook his head. "No. This is me moving on, you know? It's going to be my project, just me. I'd rather have you come with me than them."

Parker's heart threatened to burst. He was certainly reading far too much into it, but Taylor's request was stoking the little embers of his crush up into a roaring flame. Taylor wanted *him* to tag along, no one else. It had to be obvious on his face, surely—he glanced down at his laptop, too embarrassed to look Taylor in the eye.

"Y-Yeah, of course," he stammered, nodding quickly. "Just tell me when. I'll be there."

Chapter Four
Parker

The week passed by far slower than Parker would have liked, but soon enough, it was the day they were set to go check out the old venue with Zed. They planned to meet downtown for coffee first, then walk over to the venue. Somehow a bundle of nerves—despite how often he told himself that it was only Taylor, and they were meeting as friends—Parker arrived at the coffee shop far too early and was already on his second latte by the time Taylor walked in.

"Hey," he said breathlessly as Taylor joined him. "Good to see you."

"Hi," Taylor replied, and to Parker's surprise, he leaned over and gave him a quick hug. It was a friendly, one-armed hug, but it still sent thrills of electricity shooting through his body. Had they always hugged when they met? Somehow, he couldn't remember. "Hope you weren't waiting too long."

"Huh?" Parker replied stupidly, then shook himself. "Oh, uh, no, not at all. No worries."

Taylor stifled a wry grin. "You couldn't have ordered my drink for me?"

Parker laughed. "I'd probably mess up your order. I only ever order a latte. If that's what you want, then I could've ordered, but..."

"It's not *that* complicated," Taylor protested, then stepped to the counter and ordered his nonfat white mocha with no whipped cream.

"Not that complicated," Parker agreed wryly as they stepped away from the counter. His stomach fluttered when Taylor laughed in response.

"Ready?" Taylor asked once his drink was done, and Parker nodded. Together, they walked out of the coffee shop and toward the venue, which was only a few blocks away. Though he'd seemed cheerful in the coffee shop, Taylor was mostly quiet as they walked. He wore sunglasses outside, so Parker couldn't get a clear look at his face when he snuck a few sidelong glances at the other man. He couldn't say for sure, but he guessed Taylor was nervous. That made sense, he supposed: he would have to decide soon if he really wanted to buy the venue or not, which was a big decision.

He wasn't sure what to say, or if he should say anything at all, so they walked side by side in silence for a block or two. Then, finally, he asked cautiously,

"How have you been holding up?"

Taylor's nose wrinkled in a grimace, and he took a sip of his drink before he answered. "I've been okay. It comes and goes, you know?" Parker nodded, and Taylor continued, "I keep meaning to set another appointment to get this stupid cast off, but... I don't know. I always remember after the office is closed, and then I hate leaving a message and playing phone tag."

"I can help if you want," Parker offered. "Like if you need me to make an appointment, or take you, or something... Just let me know."

Taylor pulled a different face at that, one that left Parker couldn't make sense of. But after a beat, he replied, "Yeah, maybe. I'll let you know."

The venue was in sight now as they crossed the street, and Parker could see Zed Miller leaning against the wall, waiting for them. The man must have been in his sixties now—he'd been much older than them even when Get Well Soon played their first show there a decade ago. He was a tall man with a full head of gray hair and tattoos covering his arms; without the tattoos, though, he might have looked like any old man off the street, not the owner of what had once been one of the most popular indie rock venues in San Diego.

Zed looked up from his phone as they approached and grinned.

"Good to see you, Taylor," he said, starting to reach out to shake his hand, before seeming to catch himself and grabbing his shoulder instead. "How're you holding up? Who's your friend?"

"Hey, Zed," Taylor chuckled as Zed patted his shoulder. "I'm doing alright. You know Parker Flores from Punk News Net?"

"Oh, Parker! Of course," Zed said apologetically, extending his hand to Parker. "That's right. Boy, it's been years since I've seen you in person, hasn't it?"

"No worries," Parker replied, shaking his hand. "It's been a while since I've covered a live event, to be honest. Tim has me mostly doing album reviews and artist interviews these days. But it's good to see you."

"Good to see you," Zed repeated, then gestured for them to follow as he turned to the door of the empty venue. "Well, let me show you around. C'mon in, both of you."

The doors creaked loudly as he pushed them open, leading into a walkway that had once been covered in cymbals and drum heads signed by bands that had performed there, but the walls were now bare and dusty.

Bittersweet nostalgia filled Parker's chest as they walked through the short hallway—skipping the bathrooms and the entrance to the box office off to the side—and out onto the main floor.

The Bridge was fairly small, but standing there in the empty room made the stage seem almost pathetically tiny. Had entire bands fit on the small raised rectangle on the far side of the room, jumping and screaming and singing? He had such vivid memories of being up at the front—inches away from lead singers and guitarists with no barricade to separate them, covered in sweat and spit and loving every second of it. The whole world could have fit in the room then; everything worth caring about right in front of him, crowded around him, and singing along.

Now the stage was empty, and a wooden panel near the front had been ripped off entirely, leaving splinters and shards of wood sticking out at all angles. Scrapes and scuffs littered the wood floor; it would need to be refinished at a bare minimum, but Parker wondered if it would be more worth it to tear it out and replace it altogether. He could just make out the small balcony opposite the stage that had once been a VIP seating area, but it looked like all the chairs and tables had been removed. Beneath it, the bar looked alright, but surely the appliances were as old and worn as everything else. And they hadn't even seen the green room, which overlooked the main floor and was only accessible from a private staircase backstage; he was sure it had endured all sorts of abuse over the years and would also be in poor shape.

It wouldn't be impossible, but it was a *lot*. Definitely more than Taylor could manage on his own, especially if his arm was still in the cast for much longer.

He glanced over at Taylor, who, to his surprise, was smiling as he surveyed the open space, blue eyes bright and shining. It made all his worry vanish at once. If Taylor was happy with it, then surely it was perfect.

"Stage's busted, as you can see," Zed sighed, folding his arms over his chest. "All the flooring probably needs to be replaced, too, to be honest. Everything else's old, but still works. I tossed all the bar equipment; but there's a fridge, freezer, convection oven, and a dishwashing setup in the back that should still all be up to code—they aren't pretty, but they work."

"How's the green room?" Parker asked, glancing up at the single window dubiously.

"Carpet's thrashed," Zed admitted. "But that's about it. The bathroom up there's still in pretty good shape, if you can believe it. The downstairs bathrooms... Well, they work, but they probably need some fixing up, too."

"That's doable," Taylor said firmly, still looking around. "That's all doable."

Zed laughed. "That's what I want to hear."

"Why'd you close it down, Zed?" Parker asked. He remembered seeing the news that the Bridge would be closing, but it had all been vague without a reason that Parker could discern.

Zed sighed. "To be honest, I was burnt out. My wife got sick, and taking care of her and both venues were too much for me. Our other venue in North Park was performing better and has a bigger staff, so I decided to close down the Bridge—handed over a lot of the day to day of the Harmony Theater to the staff too. Kim's doing a lot better now, but we're ready to step back more permanently. I thought maybe we'd rebrand and reopen, but..."

He sighed again, looking over the space with his hands on his hips. Parker nodded quietly, peering over at the older man and trying to read his inscrutable expression.

"Can we see upstairs?" Taylor asked, and Zed nodded, shaking himself from his reverie.

"C'mon up," he said, and they headed for the stairs.

Overall, the venue was largely just as Zed described—not in great shape, but Parker supposed the repairs *were* doable. Probably. Maybe with a few contractors helping out. Something told him Taylor wasn't quite as realistic, though, judging from the same sparkle that flashed in his eyes with each part of the venue that they inspected. By the time they'd toured upstairs, backstage, then arrived back down in the pit right in front of the stage, Parker had no doubt Taylor was going to go through with it after all.

Parker glanced over at Taylor as the three of them stood in silence, looking around the room once again. Both he and Zed had distant, wistful expressions. Parker wondered what he might be thinking about. Was he worried about the amount of work renovating the venue would require? Or did he already have a vision for what it would look like under his ownership?

If anything, he was sure Taylor was thinking about Zach, wondering what he might have thought about all this; or thinking about how, if Zach were still here, they wouldn't be in this position at all.

He needed to get out of his head about it all. Taylor asked him there because they were friends, and Parker needed to stop reading so much into it.

"Thanks for showing us around," Taylor said after a beat of silence, pulling Parker's attention back to him. "Send me over the paperwork, and I'll have my lawyer look over it, but I'm feeling pretty good about this, Zed."

Zed beamed at him, and Parker couldn't help but smile, too. For all his own concerns, it was heartening to hear

Taylor feeling so positive about something—anything, really—after the past few months he'd had. If Taylor was happy about this, then so was he.

"Sounds good," Zed agreed, patting Taylor's shoulder. "I'll email you tonight. Take your time looking everything over, alright? No rush for any of this. I know it's been a rough couple of months for you. I'm in no hurry, so you don't need to be either, okay?"

Taylor flashed him a small, wry smile. His eyes briefly flickered over to Parker. He could have sworn the other man's gaze visibly softened before he looked back at Zed, making Parker's heart skip a beat. He really was seeing things now, he was sure.

"Thanks, Zed," Taylor said. "I will."

The older man turned to Parker. "And it was nice to see you, too, Parker. I'm glad you're helping Taylor out. God knows he needs good people around him right now."

Parker smiled in return. "Yeah, of course. I'm happy to help. It's been good to see you, too."

They shuffled back out to the hall and out the front door, then said their goodbyes. Taylor seemed to hesitate for a long moment, watching Zed walk in the opposite direction while biting his lower lip.

"Thanks for coming," he finally said, looking at Parker. "It made me feel a lot better to have you here."

Parker grinned despite himself. "I barely did anything. That was all you."

"Moral support," Taylor chuckled, glancing back at The Bridge one last time before turning to Parker again. "I don't have any plans after this. Want to get lunch?"

For all that he'd tried to keep his unruly heart in check, something in Parker leapt in joy at the offer.

"Yeah!" he said, far too enthusiastically, so he turned away and coughed. "Sorry, I—I mean, yeah, of course. Any particular place in mind?"

Taylor's eyes softened again. "Surprise me."

Chapter Five
Taylor

Parker ended up choosing a nearby Mexican place that was still serving brunch. Taylor's chest had been tight with anxiety the whole time, so when the waitress took their drink orders and Parker ordered a beer, Taylor added quickly,

"And I'll do a strawberry margarita."

Parker blinked owlishly at him in surprise from across the table, making him look away self-consciously, as the waitress cheerfully complimented his choice and hurried away. After a beat, Parker asked in a careful tone,

"Are, uh, are you drinking now?"

Taylor bit back a laugh. "Well, not really, but... I mean, I really only stopped drinking to help Zach when he got sober. Now... So it's fine now."

Parker was obviously trying to hide his concerned expression, but wasn't doing a very good job. This time, Taylor really did laugh.

"This is actually the first time I've had a drink since we quit, I swear," he added, grinning over at Parker. "You don't have to worry about me, really. I'm not secretly drinking at home or anything. Promise."

Parker managed a slight smile. "Alright. Just don't overdo it, okay?"

"I won't," Taylor agreed.

They sat in silence for a little while as they looked over the menu. It was getting late for breakfast food, but the restaurant was still serving pancakes and waffles, which was sorely tempting. What would go well with a strawberry margarita? He hadn't had any alcohol since Zach had given it up years ago, so even though he'd made the decision in the spur of the moment, it suddenly felt like a big deal.

He could feel Parker's gaze on him; but when he glanced up, the other man's eyes darted away quickly, looking back down at his menu.

There was so *much* he wanted to say, but it was all competing to be the first to come out of his mouth, leaving him mute with indecision. Parker's endearingly flustered expression—obviously trying to look like he hadn't been watching Taylor and failing—made warmth rise from his chest up to his face.

When Parker eventually looked up at him again, Taylor blurted out the first thing he could think of:

"So I have to tell Dean and Angie that I'm not doing music anymore."

Parker gave a slight start, obviously not expecting the confession—Taylor winced internally, not entirely having expected it either. It was one of the things that he'd wanted to talk about, sure, but adding another thing to the pile of worries that Parker was helping him through seemed like a mistake. It was what had come out, though, so he waited nervously as Parker seemed to process the words.

"I'm, uh, I'm surprised you haven't told them yet," Parker finally answered. "It seemed like you already decided."

"I just... didn't know how to bring it up," Taylor replied. "But I know I have to. I'm having the band over tomorrow for dinner to... talk."

"That's good," Parker said encouragingly.

"And I've thought about what you said about the charity show, too," Taylor continued. "I'll tell them that, too, and see what they think. Will you... Will you be there? I'm really nervous about it."

Parker's eyes widened—in the early afternoon sun, they were a warm honeyed brown that made Taylor's pulse quicken. His mouth worked silently for a brief instant, then he stammered out,

"Yeah, of course. You said it's tomorrow night?"

Taylor nodded. "Yeah, at my place. Can you come?"

"Yeah, I don't have plans. I'll be there."

For what felt like the first time in days, maybe weeks—maybe months—Taylor smiled. Not one of the small, forced smiles that were all he could manage most days. It was a real, wide, genuine smile that made his eyes crinkle and his cheeks hurt. Knowing Parker would be there made him feel so relieved and happy and... and something else he couldn't describe, but it made the looming conversation feel far less daunting.

Parker blinked hard, color rising rapidly in his face, then after a beat he smiled back, still meeting Taylor's gaze.

His sweet smile made Taylor feel like he might burst, so he looked away, still grinning stupidly. Luckily, the waitress came by with their drinks at that moment, placing the light beer in front of Parker and the wide cup full of pink slush in front of Taylor.

"Ready to order?" she chirped as Taylor busied himself with flipping through the menu again.

"You go first," he said to Parker, who nodded, still smiling.

"I'll just do the breakfast burrito," he said, and the waitress nodded sagely.

"Good choice," she said, then looked at Taylor.

"The cinnamon roll pancakes," he said decisively, and she grinned.

"Those are my *favorite*," she said in a conspiratorial whisper, making him chuckle. As she stepped away, Parker shot him an amused look over the glass of his beer.

"Pancakes, huh?" he chuckled, and Taylor shrugged. "You and your sweet tooth. Those do sound great, though, to be honest."

Taylor nodded, but he was staring down at the margarita in front of him. When Zach had finally decided to get sober, Taylor had promised to stay sober with him, too, in solidarity and support. He'd never had a problem with alcohol, but Zach was notorious for throwing himself completely into whatever he did, vices included. There was no need to abstain now, but it still felt strange—a finality to that part of his life.

He pulled the heavy glass up to take a long, slow sip. It was cold and sweet and refreshing: a hit of strawberry first before the bite of the tequila, which made his eyes water. The first sip made him cough, setting the cup down so he wouldn't spill. The burn was already fading, but his eyes still watered.

"You alright?" Parker asked, his tone concerned, as Taylor coughed and cleared his throat. His eyes were burning, and he wiped them hurriedly. He'd cried so often in the past months that he almost didn't register the tears blurring his vision—it wasn't the alcohol, but the swell of mixed emotions that burst to the surface of his consciousness when the taste of it hit his tongue. "Oh—Taylor."

His name hung in the air between them. He was sure Parker was starting to say something like, *it's okay* or *don't cry*, but caught himself. Instead, it was only those two words that came out. *Oh. Taylor.*

"I'm—I'm okay," he croaked, shaking his head. "Sorry. I don't know... It just feels like a lot. Final. You know?"

Parker was silent for a long moment. When Taylor's eyes stopped watering, he glanced up nervously at the other man again, but Parker's expression was only one of concern and care. He wasn't pulling away—he wasn't uncomfortable. Maybe, Taylor thought, he did somehow understand what Taylor meant, despite the mess of words he'd used to unsuccessfully describe it.

"Yeah," Parker finally replied, his voice just above a whisper. He didn't say anything else, but reached across the table and squeezed Taylor's left wrist, the one not in the cast. It was a short, tight, supportive squeeze, but somehow it felt unfathomably intimate, enough to make him feel like his face was burning.

"It's... It's really good, though," Taylor finally forced out. Parker stared at him for a moment, then chuckled, the smile breaking across his features with relief. Taylor took another sip, and this time it felt like a weight being released from his body. Cold, and sweet, and refreshing. "Yeah. It's good."

Parker's gaze was soft and affectionate now. "Told you this place was good."

What if he just told Parker now? Taylor's heart started pounding. He wanted to tell him—to tell him *everything*—but if one sip of a margarita could make him tear up, maybe it would be better to wait. No, now wasn't ideal. It could wait. It would have to.

Instead, he smiled in return. "You were right."

//

When he got home later that afternoon, Taylor stood in the entryway of the house for a long, long moment, staring across the hall into the living room. So much of Zach's stuff was already packed away, but there was still a half-filled duffel bag of clothes in the closet, and a pile of random books and electronics in their studio. Even without seeing them, Taylor knew they were still there—could feel their presence acutely, like splinters stuck in his skin. He hadn't had the heart to finish packing them away yet.

But something in him had changed at brunch. No, it had started sooner than that—it had started when he stood in the empty pit of The Bridge, remembering the first show they'd every played on that stage and simultaneously imagining what it would be like when it was his. It was the first time he could clearly see what his future could be like without the band, without his life orbiting around Zach and his gravitational magnetism.

He ended up in the studio first, staring at all their recording equipment and keyboards that made a maze of the room. He could get rid of it all. What good was any of this to him now?

On the desk that had once housed Zach's computer, there was a clear plastic bin that had a few assorted microphones and guitar pedals, some notebooks with scribbled lyrics that had never made it out of the brainstorming stage, a mess of tangled aux cords, and some self-help books. Taylor could still so clearly see Zach curled up on the couch with one of those books in his lap, eyes locked on it with the intensity of a man who truly believed it might hold the key to fixing everything wrong in his life.

He'd been obsessed with these sorts of books when he got sober; Taylor didn't think he'd ever seen Zach re-read one, though. He didn't know how much they'd ever helped him, if at all. But he could still clearly see Zach here—his dark hair pushed back messily, the small tattoo under his eye crinkled and distorted as he squinted in concentration—and despite everything, it made Taylor's heart squeeze to remember.

Taylor turned away from the box of stuff that he still had to get rid of, instead scanning the walls. He didn't play guitar, so he'd probably give them all over to Kylie or Angie, or sell some of them. There were some mounted special editions of their albums and the handful of awards they'd won—those he might give to the other members of the band, too.

There was only one thing he really wanted to keep. Carefully mounted in a small frame, the handwritten lyrics of Wish We Were There hung on the wall above the desk where Zach used to work. The final version of the song had changed a bit, but this was the first iteration of the song that had launched them into fame and success. It didn't look special. He'd written it in pencil on lined paper ripped out of a 99-cent notebook that they had probably picked up from a drugstore somewhere in the Midwest while on tour. The paper was marked with both Zach's messy scrawl and

Taylor's more careful handwriting; Zach had written the opening and the bridge, and Taylor had come up with the chorus. He didn't even remember where they were when they'd worked on the song—here at home, or on the tour bus, or maybe even some random cafe or diner in another state that he would never visit again.

But he knew what he'd been feeling when he wrote the lyrics. Maybe he'd already known then how things were changing. *Baby, don't you wish we were there?*

With newfound resolve, he finished packing. He took the pedals out of the box—Angie had her own preferred pedals, but he figured she should get first pick before he sold them—and filled the rest of it with remaining cords and books, until he could barely get the locking clip over the lid to keep it closed.

"Sorry, babe," he said softly once it was done, then carried it out into the garage. The last of his clothes were next, tossed haphazardly into a bag before joining the box. Tomorrow, he'd take it to the donation center, drop it off, and never see any of it again. Then everything in the house would be his, before the rest of the band came for dinner. Before Parker was here. Something in that felt refreshing, somehow.

Bittersweet, he thought, closing the garage door behind him. *There's a lyric there somewhere.* But he shook the idea away before his mind could start puzzling it out. He was done with music, with songs, with the band. And Zach. He didn't need any of it anymore.

Chapter Six
Parker

This is so stupid. It's dinner with the band, not a date.

Dinner with Taylor and the rest of the band was in less than an hour, and Parker had spent the last forty minutes staring at himself in the mirror and trying different outfits. Despite how much he repeated to himself that he was overthinking this, none of the things that he would usually wear seemed right. His go-to dressed up outfit was too nice; something more casual felt too flippant. Texting Taylor to ask him about a dress code was entirely out of the question—he was sure no one was thinking about it as hard as he was.

And then there was the matter of his hair. Short and dark brown with a tiny hint of a natural wave when it started getting a little long; he rarely gave it a second thought, but sometimes he wore it all pushed to one side, and sometimes he wore it slicked back. It was at a length now where the waviness wasn't really visible, but he could always squish some mousse into the length to help accentuate it—or should he just wear it to the side like normal? He had a little bit of scruff, too, but in his panic ended up shaving his face.

In the end, he left his apartment five minutes later than he'd meant to: clean-shaven with his hair pushed to the side with pomade, wearing a gray and black patterned button-down shirt, black jeans, and his brown leather jacket draped over one arm to ward off the outdoor autumn chill.

It wasn't his nicest outfit, but it would be nice enough for a dinner party. Hopefully. Maybe he should have just worn a nice t-shirt instead, something less formal...

He'd aimed to arrive a bit early, but as he parked in front of Taylor's house, he saw that Kylie had arrived at the same time. She noticed him as she was getting out of her car and waved at him with a smile. He managed a smile back and waved in return. She was wearing a black dress with straps around the neckline that created the shape of a pentagram underneath a black-and-white checkered cardigan. Her outfits always looked perfectly put together, but he was relieved to see that she was dressed relatively casually, so his outfit wouldn't be out of place.

"Stop freaking out," he hissed to his reflection in the rearview mirror, before getting out of the car and jogging across the street to join Kylie, a canvas tote bag slung over her shoulder. Should he have brought something? Taylor told him that he was having dinner catered, so there was no need to bring anything, but it definitely looked like Kylie brought something.

"Hey, Parker," she said with a wide grin. "I didn't know you were part of the dinner party."

"Oh," he said, surprised. "Er, yeah. Taylor invited me. I hope that's okay?"

She laughed. "I mean, it's his house. I just didn't realize. It's good to see you."

There was something sly in the way that she smiled at him as they walked up to the front door, but he was too anxious about Taylor to give it much consideration. He reached for the doorbell, but Kylie pushed right past him and opened the door.

"We're here!" she called out cheerfully. "You didn't tell me you were inviting *Parker*!"

Taylor's voice came from the kitchen. "Come on in. And, oh, yeah, I invited Parker."

"I'm here too," Parker called nervously, hovering in the doorway as Kylie waltzed through. Taylor appeared from the kitchen, smiling first at her, then across the hallway at Parker.

For a moment, they both stood there, motionless, looking at each other with slight smiles. *Why am I so pathetic?* Parker thought, everything in him melting at the sight of the other man. His blond hair was tucked behind his ears, and he wore an oversized mustard yellow sweater over a collared shirt and light jeans, his feet bare. He looked so cozy and homey and *comforting*, like a warm mug of apple cider.

Taylor's smile became shy as he glanced away—Parker was sure he was imagining the faint flush rising in the other man's cheeks. "Don't just stand there, dude. C'mon."

"Right, yeah," he stammered, hurriedly pulling his shoes off and setting them on the shoe rack by the doorway. Kylie hadn't bothered with her Converse, and Taylor didn't seem to care; but he could always hear his mother in the back of his head, chiding him not to wear shoes indoors. "I didn't bring anything. I hope that's okay?"

"Yeah, of course," Taylor replied. "I got everything, so no worries."

"I just brought wine 'cause I figured we were gonna need it," Kylie called from the kitchen.

Taylor nodded, and Parker breathed a sigh of relief.

"So when's everyone else getting here?" he asked, following Taylor to the kitchen.

"Any minute now," Taylor replied, glancing at the clock. "I'm sure Dean and Angie will come together. She can drive again now, but I'd be surprised if they turn up separately." He hesitated, shooting Parker a furtive glance. "They're, uh... The only ones who don't know so far."

Despite his hushed tone, Kylie whirled on them with a scandalized expression. "Seriously, Taylor, you told him before you told them?"

Parker's heart sunk into his stomach at her tone, but Taylor only huffed and waved her away.

"Sorry I talk to people other than you, Kylie," he muttered, but Parker could tell he was fighting down a smile. Kylie's answering scoff sounded just as good-natured, filling him with relief. The last thing he wanted was to cause any sort of divide between Taylor and the rest of the band, all things considered.

"Oh, god, Parker, stop looking like such a lost puppy!" Kylie exclaimed. "Don't be freaked out, okay? This is just how we are. Everyone loves you already. Seriously, when was the last time we hung out?"

"Uh, I'm not sure," Parker replied, laughing nervously. Nothing she was saying was making him feel any better, though he supposed it was meant to be reassuring. Taylor shot her an unreadable look, and her expression morphed rapidly over several seconds, until finally she chirped out,

"You know what, I'm going to go set out some wine glasses. Excuse me."

She bustled past him carrying several wine glasses by their stems, leaving Parker bewildered in the middle of the kitchen with Taylor looking uncomfortable, as he busied himself with pulling plates out of the cabinet.

"What—What was that about?" Parker asked, half-laughing, and Taylor let out a strained noise in response.

"She has this idea that..." he started, then trailed off, waving a hand dismissively. "You know, never mind. It's stupid. I don't know how to explain. Ignore her. Listen, when Dean and Angie get here..."

Parker waited, but Taylor only trailed off again, his face pinching with frustration. "I... Um, will you just sit next to me?"

Somehow, he was sure that this wasn't what Taylor wanted to say when he started talking, but Parker still smiled in return, hoping he looked more confident and unperturbed than he felt.

"Yeah, of course," he replied quickly.

Taylor answered with a small, tired smile. "Thanks."

The Gomez siblings let themselves in the way Kylie had, arriving a few minutes later, just as Parker was helping Taylor carry trays of food into the dining room. Like Kylie, they both looked surprised to see him there. Angie seemed to recover quickly, though, and greeted him affably; but Dean only gave him a quick nod with an almost suspicious look on his face, leaving Parker more confused than before.

The siblings were quite different; Dean, the drummer, looked like a poster child for Hot Topic straight out of 2008: a tall, lanky twenty-something with dark hair half covering his face, stretched earlobes, a t-shirt with an indecipherable band name emblazoned across it, and black skinny jeans with a studded belt and a wallet chain. Angie, who'd played lead guitar, was dressed in a bright yellow and orange sweater and flared jeans, with dangling gold earrings that were only occasionally visible through the curtain of her jet black bob cut. Even with the heels of her ankle boots, she was a head shorter than everyone else.

Parker knew Angie did some music under her own name on the side that sounded much more like her sweet girl-next-door appearance, and he wondered what Dean would do after this was all said and done.

"Thanks for coming, everyone," Taylor said, coming out of the kitchen to usher everyone into the dining room. "Sorry I've been kind of MIA lately. Here's my peace offering."

Angie smiled. "No worries, Taylor. I'm just glad to see you."

"How's your ankle?" he asked.

"Good as new," she chuckled, sticking her booted foot out. "Is your wrist okay? I got my cast off a few weeks ago, so I'm surprised to see you still wearing it."

Taylor held his arm self-consciously closer to his body. "Yeah, all good. I missed my appointment to get it off and haven't gotten around to rescheduling."

"Gosh, isn't it killing you? Mine was so itchy, I was counting down the days to get it off."

"It's been alright," Taylor chuckled. "I'll get it off soon. Just need to reschedule."

Everyone started to sit down around the dining room table. Parker awkwardly stepped out of place so that he could sit next to Taylor as he'd asked; but he could practically *feel* the weird look Dean shot at him as they all settled into their seats. Luckily, Kylie spoke cheerfully before he could think too much about it.

"I brought wine!" she chirped, pouring the red into glasses without asking who wanted one. "No offense, Taylor. Just figured we'd need something to lighten the mood a little bit."

"I'll take some," Taylor replied, shrugging. Kylie raised an eyebrow, but offered him a glass all the same.

"We've been worried about you," Dean said, speaking for the first time. He was the quietest of the group; the deep resonance of his voice always surprised Parker whenever he did speak up. "What have you been up to, Taylor?"

Taylor shook his head. "Not much, to be honest. A lot of wallowing and feeling sorry for myself. But I'm ready to move on from that, you know? I got sick of moping. So here I am."

For some reason, everyone seemed to glance furtively at Parker the longer Taylor spoke, but he didn't know why. Were they still confused by his presence? But then why would they be looking over at him now, as if trying to gauge his reaction to Taylor's words? It wasn't adding up—clearly they were looking for *something*, but he didn't know what. He took another nervous drink of the wine. Whatever. He was here to be Taylor's moral support, so if they thought him being there was weird, they'd just have to deal with it.

"Don't rush yourself, Taylor," Angie finally spoke, her tone much more gentle. "It's a complicated situation, so... Take it easy on yourself."

"Right," Taylor agreed hurriedly, clearly trying to change the subject. "Anyway, uh, the curry and the pad thai are vegan for you, Angie, and the fried rice has shrimp. Everything else has chicken. Go ahead and serve yourselves."

"We need some music," Kylie said firmly, then called out more loudly, "Hey, Google! Play the new Blink-182 album!"

Despite himself, Parker laughed as the music came on. "New Blink, huh? Is this the kinda stuff you listen to over dinner?"

"Are you telling me you *haven't* listened to the new Blink album?" Kylie asked, her voice accusing, but with a teasing lilt.

"Oh, I've listened to it plenty. My review for it for PNN went up last week."

The mood lightened considerably as they started eating, but Parker still couldn't shake the feeling that Angie and especially Dean were watching him far too closely. Not that he had any idea why. He'd been friends with Zach and Taylor for years—while he had never exactly been a permanent fixture, the three of them would meet up with and without the rest of the band a few times a year. And Taylor would want his friends around him as much as possible, wouldn't he? So why was his presence so strange to them?

He kept thinking it over through the course of the meal, trying his best to not appear too obviously distracted. Once everyone seemed like they were mostly done, though, Taylor cleared his throat, before saying hesitantly,

"I, uh, I wanted to talk to you guys about something, actually."

Again, Dean's eyes darted straight to Parker; and this time he couldn't quite stop himself from shooting Dean an annoyed, confused expression when their eyes met. The stoic drummer didn't react, but after a beat, looked back at Taylor without speaking.

"Sure," Angie offered, sounding uncertain now too. "What's up?"

Beneath the table, Parker felt Taylor's hands first rest on his thigh, then squeeze tightly. He froze, willing himself desperately not to react outwardly, even though the firm grip of Taylor's fingers sent electricity rocketing through his nerves. Taylor was scared and nervous about this, so he needed to be strong—if this was how he needed Parker to support him, then he'd do it, and pointedly ignore how his dick was already half-hard in response.

"I, uh," Taylor stammered. "I'm buying the old Bridge, the venue Zed Miller used to own. I'm going to open a new venue there."

Everything was silent for a beat, and Taylor's fingers relaxed on Parker's leg. He finally sucked in a breath, not realizing that he'd been holding it since Taylor had first grabbed his leg. Luckily, Angie gasped at the same moment Parker did, so it didn't seem too obvious.

"Oh, what?" she exclaimed, a grin spreading across her face. "Taylor, that's *sick*. Awesome!"

Parker blinked, still trying to process. That hadn't been exactly what he'd expected Taylor to say, but it would segue into the rest well enough, he supposed. Taylor's grip had relaxed, but his hand still rested on Parker's thigh. Part of him wanted to place his own hand over Taylor's to comfort him; but maybe that would only make it worse, so he clenched both his hands into fists and kept them firmly at his sides.

"Yeah, I figured a change of pace would be good for me," Taylor continued, still sounding breathless. "And it was such a bummer when the Bridge closed... I heard Zed was selling it, and I knew I needed to act on it, you know?"

Kylie was watching Taylor, as if she too was unsure why this was what Taylor had led with. Angie was still all smiles, but Dean seemed to immediately pick up on how Parker and Kylie appeared surprised for a different reason.

"Seems like it might take up a lot of your time," he said, his voice even. "Are you still gonna have enough time for the band?"

Taylor's grip tightened around Parker's leg again, somehow even harder than before—Parker could feel his hand start to tremble, could hear it in his wavering voice as he replied,

"Well, that's the other thing. I'm... I think I'm done with the band, guys."

This time the silence dragged on for several seconds with everyone's eyes locked on Taylor, who was looking firmly down at his empty plate. His grip on Parker's thigh was becoming painful; more out of reflex than anything, Parker's hand went to grab Taylor's and give a reassuring squeeze. Taylor tensed at the contact; but before Parker could pull his hand away self-consciously, the death grip on his thigh relaxed and Taylor's fingers interlaced with his own instead.

Parker was sure the flush that rose in his face would be visible to everyone else if they bothered to look—but luckily, they all still seemed focused entirely on Taylor.

"Seriously, dude?" Dean finally scowled, and his sister reached over and smacked his shoulder hard. "Ouch! Angie, what the fuck?"

"Don't say it like that!" Angie replied, frowning at her brother, but her eyes were suddenly glassy. "It's not—It's not a surprise, okay? We already talked about how this might happen. Don't be a dick about it, Dean."

"Do you know how many people would kill to be in our position?" Dean replied sullenly, glancing between Angie and Taylor. "Taylor, we *made it*. Do you really want to throw it all away now?"

"Zach was half the appeal of the band," Kylie interrupted, making Dean roll his eyes. "I'm serious, guys. Without

Zach, the band would never be the same anyway. That's just the reality of it. Even if he didn't write almost every song, it's still all in *his* voice. There was no guarantee we were gonna make it past this, anyway. Taylor's just seeing the writing on the wall."

Angie wiped her eyes, sniffling loudly. "No, you're right. And we had the same thoughts. Zach was... I mean, I guess all bands are like this. Yeah. I'm really sorry to hear that, though, Taylor. I love making music with you guys. I'm just sad it's really over."

"Well, Parker had a great idea for one last show," Taylor said, his voice still shaking. Parker flinched at being addressed—so far he'd just been a fly on the wall, but Taylor saying his name brought him back into the conversation all at once. "Once the new venue is open... Maybe we could do a charity show, or something like that. One last hurrah to make sure everyone's taken care of before we officially end it, you know?"

Angie smiled, but somehow Dean looked even more displeased at that.

"Everyone, huh?" he asked, and the mood in the room seemed to change completely. Angie's brow furrowed, and Kylie huffed in annoyance, folding her arms across her chest. Both looked over at Taylor—some unspoken question in their eyes—who released Parker's hand all at once, inexplicably shying away from him. Parker glanced over at him, confused, but Taylor wouldn't meet his gaze. He looked askance at the others, but Dean and Angie's expressions told him nothing—Kylie seemed to flinch at his gaze and gave a tiny shake of her head.

There was something going on only the band knew about—despite his curiosity, it clearly made Taylor uncomfortable, so he held back the questions brimming on the tip of his tongue.

"You know what I mean," Taylor finally said, his voice small as he shot Dean a stern look. "Everyone, yeah."

Dean scoffed, then shrugged.

"Yeah, okay," he said. "One last show sounds good to me."

"Definitely," Angie agreed firmly. "Count us in. Do you have an idea of when?"

Taylor barked out a nervous laugh. "Not at all. I don't even have the keys yet, and there are some renovations that need to happen before we can start thinking of booking shows. So don't post or say anything about it yet. But I'll keep everyone updated for sure."

"Who will sing?" Kylie asked softly. Taylor glanced at her, then at the others.

"We all can," he replied, just as faint. "We've all done backup vocals at some point, right? We'll all sing together."

Angie managed a watery smile. "Yeah. That's sweet. Parker, that was your idea?"

"Oh, uh," Parker stammered, taken aback. "The show was my idea, that's all. Everything else is all Taylor."

Angie smiled at him, her expression warm now. Somehow that was even more confusing—why was everyone flip-flopping about him right in front of his face? "It's a good idea. Thank you."

"You're welcome," he replied, forcing himself to smile in response, despite his confusion. "I'm happy to help however I can."

For a moment, everyone was silent, then Kylie stood abruptly.

"I'll get started on these dishes," she said. Angie and Dean followed her out, leaving him and Taylor alone. He glanced at Parker with an almost guilty expression as he stood, as if he knew how confused Parker must have been, but still he didn't say anything.

"What was that about?" Parker whispered once they were alone. Taylor grimaced.

"It's complicated," he replied hurriedly. "I... I don't know how to explain, Parker. We can talk about it later. Okay?"

Parker was silent for a moment, trying to get a read on anything about what had happened from Taylor's expression, but he was still entirely at a loss.

"Okay," he finally relented, and he stood, too. "I'll help with the leftovers."

"Wait," Taylor said quickly. "I also wanted to ask you... You'll help me, right? With the renovations and stuff? Is that okay?"

Parker blinked, taken aback at the sudden change in subject. "What do you mean?"

Taylor lifted his arm in the cast self-consciously. "I won't be able to do a lot by myself, but I want to get started as soon as possible. I'll probably hire someone to put in new floors and maybe fix the stage; but everything else, I think I can do myself. Will you help me?"

Despite his apprehension, Parker managed a slight smile at Taylor's worried face. If that was how he could support Taylor, then he'd do it gladly.

"Yeah," he said, and Taylor's expression softened with a smile, too. "Yeah, of course. Just let me know when. I can probably help you find a contractor, too, for the stuff we can't do ourselves. But I'll definitely help out where I can."

"Thank you," Taylor said, relief obvious on his face. "I really appreciate it, Parker. I don't know what I'd do without you."

Heat sparked in Parker's chest at Taylor's words and the shy smile that spread across his face. He didn't know how to respond, so they just stood there smiling stupidly at each other for a moment, then Taylor gestured toward the kitchen.

"We'd better go help," he said quietly, barely above a whisper, and Parker laughed.

"You're right," he agreed, reaching to help clear the table. Some hushed conversation between Dean, Angie, and Kylie stopped abruptly as they stepped into the kitchen, but it hardly phased him now. All Parker could think of was the sweet way Taylor had looked at him when he'd agreed to help out. As long as he could keep making Taylor happy like that, nothing else mattered.

Chapter Seven
Taylor

A week later, Taylor had the keys to the venue, and his name was on the lease. His signature had been sloppy, done with his left hand; he still hadn't managed to call to have the cast taken off. It was just one more thing on a never-ending to-do list.

He hadn't seen Parker since the dinner with the rest of the band, but they'd been texting every day since then. Taylor had sent him updates about everything—signing the lease and how surreal it felt, but also smaller day-to-day things like videos that made him laugh. So far, he'd mostly been the one to text Parker first, but Parker usually responded quickly.

Parker was being a little more distant than he'd hoped, though, and Taylor kept thinking about the dinner–about the accusing look in Dean's eyes whenever he looked at Parker. He was pretty sure Parker had noticed that Dean was being so weird—and Angie too, in her own way—and he was sure it left Parker confused. But he didn't say as much, and Taylor couldn't bring himself to bring it up. It seemed like way too serious a conversation to have over text, especially considering half the messages they shared were memes or silly videos.

On Friday, he texted Parker to ask if he'd be free the next day to start cleaning things up in the Bridge now that everything was official. The other man hadn't responded right away, so his eventual reply made Taylor even more disappointed.

Parker

> Sorry dude, I'll be in LA all day tomorrow for an interview. Can we do Sunday instead?

The text felt like a rejection, which Taylor knew was unreasonable. Even though Parker was around a lot, he was still a busy person with a successful job that relied on either traveling to other people, or hosting them for interviews—both for his podcast and for Punk News Net. Texting him the day before he wanted to start was short-sighted. He should have known Parker would be busy that weekend.

Had any of their texts even been about anything Parker was doing? Did he really only talk about *himself?* Taylor groaned, inwardly berating himself. Had he ever been this pathetic when he and Zach had been talking?

No, everything with Zach had been so completely different—like a whirlwind that had caught fire. They'd barely known each other before they got together, so there had hardly been time for Taylor to pine after him. How he felt for Parker was more like a storm rolling in, tension slowly mounting until it was all he could think about.

They really needed to talk, but he already had so much on his plate. So, instead, he replied,

Taylor

> No problem, Sunday works. See you then!

It sounded far more chipper than he felt, which was exactly what he was going for. Parker replied with two emojis: a thumbs-up and a smile. Taylor smiled stupidly at his phone for a moment, before forcing himself to put it away, feeling ridiculous at how sappy the two little pictures could make him.

But by the time Sunday rolled around, doubt had gnawed at Taylor's insides until he was entirely hollow again. He arrived at the Bridge—he needed to decide on a new name, too—earlier than he and Parker had agreed, fumbling with the keys as he let himself in. Everything inside was dusty and stale; just as grim as he felt.

He was sure Parker had only agreed to help out of pity. He felt sorry for Taylor, and that was all—Taylor asking this of him was only a burden. He couldn't even recall with certainty the last time they'd hung out before Zach died, so why the hell would Parker want to just spend time with him as a friend now?

Taylor was an idiot to even hope Parker had feelings for him. He wasn't supposed to have feelings for Parker. What was he thinking? What was he *doing?*

How long had he been standing in the middle of the pit, staring vacantly at the stage? With a groan of self-pity, he shook himself out of the stupor that he'd found himself in, though his mood remained dark as ever. Parker would be here soon, so he had to at least look busy. He started with the bar, running the sink in the back to fill it with hot, soapy water. Every surface was going to need a good cleaning, and while he had to be careful not to get the cast wet, it seemed like an easy enough task to start with.

He'd finished scrubbing down the countertops and was working on the empty ice bin when the front door clattered open. He paused, peering over the bar just in case it was some curious pedestrian who'd come inside instead of Parker. But the footfalls coming through the entry hall were familiar; Parker appeared in the hallway, making Taylor's heart jump.

"Hey!" Parker said breathlessly, a wide smile crossing his face. Even from across the room, Taylor could see the way his warm brown eyes crinkled at the edges as he smiled. His dark hair was tousled from the breeze outdoors, his face flushed from the wind.

He looked so unbearably happy to see Taylor that all the bleak thoughts that had been clouding his mind were gone in an instant. "I'm not late, am I?"

Taylor blinked, processing. "Oh, uh—no, not at all. I just wanted to get an early start."

Parker's smile remained as he stepped up toward the bar. "Good. Want me to help you with that, or are you going to put me to work somewhere else?"

Taylor laughed, shaking his head. "Why don't you take this over? I'm really not supposed to be getting the cast wet, but it's kind of tricky to avoid..."

Parker's cheerful grin finally faltered. "Shit, I said I would help you get the appointment set up, then I never did. Sorry."

"Don't apologize," Taylor replied quickly, waving the words away. "It's all on me. I keep meaning to. It's so stupid."

"Let's call right now," Parker prompted him, pulling his phone from his pocket. "So I don't forget again. What's the number?"

Taylor's heart flip-flopped painfully in his chest—that was the last thing he wanted to worry about right now. "Um, I'm not sure. I'll have to look it up, and my phone is in the back..."

He trailed off. Parker gave him an appraising look, somehow recognizing Taylor's reluctance as he put his phone in his back pocket again.

"Okay. Maybe when we take a break for lunch, then," Parker replied. "Don't let me forget again. We have *got* to get that cast off you before this place opens, you know?"

Taylor managed to laugh again. He always felt so much better when Parker was around—the other man always knew exactly what to say to make him laugh or smile when he got too much into his head—the way he'd been doing all day.

"Maybe I can just dissolve it off in the water," he joked, handing over the sponge he'd been using to scrub out the ice bin. "No appointment needed then."

Parker laughed, rolling up his sleeves. "I do *not* want to be the one to clean that up. No, let's leave it to the professionals, please."

Taylor stepped back, and Parker went right to work scrubbing out the bin. He watched for a moment, feeling heat rising in his face as his eyes lingered on the shadow Parker's eyelashes cast down his face, the way his shirt lifted a little bit to expose a sliver of his back and the waistband of his underwear as he leaned forward to reach into the deep bin.

"Hey, do you—oh," Parker stammered, turning back to look at Taylor, catching him obviously staring. Taylor glanced away, sure his face was bright red, but when he looked back, Parker looked just as flustered. "I was gonna ask, um, do you have any of those rubber cleaning gloves? Maybe those will help, you know, if you're worried about the cast getting wet and all..."

Taylor laughed nervously. "I'll have to dig around in the cleaning supplies Zed left behind to see what he has. Let me check."

His heart rate had slowed back to a normal pace once he'd looked through the back room, eventually finding a package of rubber gloves wedged into a box of paper towels. Taylor pulled one over his cast, then brought the rest to Parker.

"You were right," he chuckled as Parker took the gloves.

"So, what's the plan for the rest of the day?" Parker asked.

"I think I want to get everything clean to get a better idea of what's salvageable," Taylor sighed, looking around. "I don't want to do too much of a deep clean in case a lot of things need to be replaced, but I think once all the dust is gone, I'll have a better sense of what shape all the bar stuff is in."

"Have you talked to anyone about the floor or the stage?"

Taylor shook his head. "No, but that's on my list."

Parker nodded. "Well, let's finish up the bar and the back room, then. Sounds good?"

They got to work cleaning. Parker focused on the ice box and the fridge under the counter, while Taylor wiped down all the shelves and storage cubbies along the wall. Every so often he would sneak a glance over at Parker; and once or twice he caught Parker looking over at him, too. A weird, pleasant anticipation built up in his chest, warmth filling him as he considered maybe Parker liked watching him nearly as much as he did.

"Hey, uh," Parker said once he'd finished cleaning out the fridge, leaning against the bar and fiddling with the gloves. They were a little too big for his hands, so the fingers were floppy on the end. "About dinner the other night... I kind of noticed Dean kept, like, I don't know... Looking at me weird, I guess. Do you know what that was about?"

Taylor bit his lip, his light mood sinking quickly. "I, uh, I noticed the same thing."

"What was his problem?" Parker asked, sounding more curious than upset. "I don't really think I did anything to him. I mean, I've spoken to him maybe three times in as many years, so... I just don't know what was going on with him."

Taylor hesitated for a long moment. He wanted to tell Parker the truth, but the words caught in his throat.

"I..." he started, then trailed off, coughing. "It's a long story, to be honest, but he was just being an asshole. I don't want to get into it."

He could feel Parker's eyes lingering on him, but couldn't bring himself to turn around to face the other man. Maybe Parker was looking at him with confusion, or frustration, or even sadness; but Taylor didn't think he could keep it together if he saw any of it on Parker's face. After a moment, he heard Parker sigh.

"So you don't think I did anything to piss him off?" he asked, and Taylor shook his head.

"No, I don't think so," he replied. He risked a glance back at Parker now, since he didn't sound upset; the other man was looking at him with a resigned sort of expression, but managed a small smile when Taylor turned to look at him.

"Alright. Then I won't press," he said, holding up a hand. "If it's weird band shit, I won't try to get involved. If you say I didn't do something to make him mad, then I believe you."

Taylor chuckled, his chest squeezing at the unfiltered earnestness in Parker's voice.

"Yeah, weird band dynamic stuff," he agreed, sighing. "I figure it'll probably be like that until..."

He trailed off, unsure of how to say it. Until the band was broken up for good? Until their last performance was over, and they could part ways? None of it sounded great.

"I understand," Parker replied softly. Taylor nodded, and neither of them spoke for a while. The only sound between them was the measured scrubbing of Parker methodically working his way across the bar countertop, and the faint thud of Taylor opening and closing the various cabinets as he sprayed them down and wiped them clean.

It hadn't entirely been a lie—it *was* largely because of weird band dynamics playing out. It *was* a shift because of Zach's sudden absence, when he'd been the one holding them all together. But it didn't feel good to keep the truth from Parker, either.

"So are you still gonna call it The Bridge?" Parker finally asked, shaking Taylor from his thoughts.

"Huh?" Taylor stammered, turning back to look at him in surprise. "Oh—The Bridge. I've been thinking about it, actually, and, um, I think I have a different name in mind."

"Oh yeah?" Parker asked. His cheerful grin stopped Taylor from spiraling. He was sure Parker hadn't been dwelling on the exchange at all, in stark contrast to how he kept playing the conversation over in his head. "What were you thinking?"

Heat rose in Taylor's face, suddenly embarrassed at the change in topic. He had an idea for a new name, but hadn't yet spoken it aloud to anyone.

"Well, uh," he started, running a nervous hand through his hair. "It's not for sure, but I've been thinking something like... Well, I like the sound of *The Caesura Room*."

"Ooh," Parker said, eyebrows raising. "What does it mean?"

"Maybe it's not a good name," Taylor blurted out. "Since it's more of a classical music term... I think most people won't know what it means. Do you think that would be too confusing?"

"What? No, I like how it sounds," Parker replied. "And plenty of venues have weird names. No one will think too much about it. But what does it mean?"

"It's a kind of a pause," Taylor said. Maybe the more he said the name, the less silly it would seem. "I thought it would be nice because... Well, I'm wanting it to have a focus on LGBTQ musicians. Not just a safe space, but an explicitly queer venue, you know? Like a break from the rest of the world. So a break in the music is a caesura. I don't know. I guess it sounded nice."

The words had all left him in a rush, so he couldn't gauge Parker's reaction until he was done speaking. Would he laugh? Would he think it was as goofy as it sounded in Taylor's head?

Parker smiled, his eyes shining. "Aw, Taylor. I love that. It sounds perfect. I bet if you have a little poster or something at the entrance—explaining what a caesura is and how it's related to the venue—people are gonna love it."

Taylor's heart skipped a beat. "You really think so?"

"Hell yeah, dude! It sounds awesome. *The Caesura Room*," Parker replied, repeating the phrase to himself a few times. "Yeah, it's good. You should go with that. Unless you had other ideas?"

"That was the winner so far," Taylor admitted with a self-conscious laugh. "So, you know, if you think it's good, I'll stick with it."

He didn't think Parker's smile could widen any more, but somehow he grinned even harder in response.

"It's perfect," Parker repeated. "And now I get bragging rights that I helped name the place."

Taylor stared at him for a moment, then burst out laughing. Parker's eyes crinkled with mirth as he laughed, too.

"Definitely mention that when you write an article about the grand opening. People will eat that up," Taylor chuckled, shaking his head as he turned back to the cabinet that he'd been spraying down.

"Oh, I'm already planning it out," Parker agreed.

Chapter Eight
Parker

With everything they got done the first day, Taylor said that he thought they could get the venue ready to host performances again within six months, hopefully less. Parker had laughed, shaking his head, and bet that they could do it in half that amount of time if they put their minds to it. Taylor had only smiled shyly back at him and shrugged, giving a noncommittal reply.

But looking at all the interviews and trips he had booked already in the coming weeks and months, Parker would only be free to help around one day a week for the first few months, so maybe it would take the better part of six months after all. A daunting timeframe, but Taylor seemed unbothered by it.

"I'm not in a rush," he said, shrugging. "I'll finish it when I finish it. When I'm ready."

"You're not worried about the rest of the band getting antsy? Or fans wanting to know what's going on?" Parker asked, frowning. Taylor shook his head.

"Honestly, I'm completely off the band's social media right now," he said. "I'm really trying to avoid anything about it."

He chuckled, but his expression was pained. Parker's throat tightened with concern. He didn't press Taylor on it, though; it seemed understandably stressful to talk about, so he moved on to lighter conversation as they packed up for the day.

When he got home that evening, Parker realized that he never got the phone number to the doctor's office from Taylor. Kicking himself mentally, he texted Taylor to ask for it, but the other man didn't reply until the next day.

Taylor

> Here's the number. Schedule it
> whenever. Thanks for helping.

The soonest date the doctor's office could see him would be in two weeks, which seemed an awfully long time for Taylor to keep the cast on his arm still. The receptionist on the phone didn't seem overly concerned, just surprised that it had taken this long for him to reschedule. Luckily, Parker's schedule was clear that day, so he texted Taylor, letting him know and offering to take him, if that would help. Again, the other man didn't reply right away; but when he did, he agreed to have Parker accompany him.

Taylor

> Thanks again, dude. I really don't know what I would do without you.

Parker smiled stupidly at his phone, re-reading the message. It felt silly to get so sappy over such a mundane message, but something about the words were sweet and intimate. Much as he knew he shouldn't read too much into it, he indulged the butterflies in his stomach for a little bit at the thought that maybe Taylor's thanks might eventually grow into something more.

But it was wishful thinking, and he had a ton to do before they saw each other next. So eventually, he pushed it from his mind and sat down to work on his next article.

11

A last-minute interview disrupted Parker's plan to meet Taylor at the venue the next week.

"Can we seriously not reschedule for any other day?" Parker groaned over the phone. His boss, Tim, scoffed from the other end of the line.

"Parker, we're talking about *Jason Daugherty* here," he snapped. From the faint background noise and the distant echo of his voice, Parker could tell Tim was talking to him while he was driving. "The man hasn't done any official interviews in nearly three years. He's practically a hermit by now. His agent reached out to us saying he wants to get the word out that he's working on a new album, and it'll be a cold day in hell when I turn something like that down. Anyway, the guy would be a gay icon if he hadn't fallen off the face of the earth, so I thought you'd be happier about an opportunity like this."

Parker bit his lip, trying to tamp down his frustration. "I mean, I *am*, really, I just..."

"Parker, I promise you I wouldn't be asking you to do this if I didn't think it was important. No one else can take it on such short notice."

He remained silent for a long moment, considering. The chance to interview Jason Daugherty was one he would have accepted in a heartbeat on any other day. He had been one of the biggest up-and-coming stars in the emo revival a decade ago, but the bright trajectory of his career had fizzled out abruptly following the messy public breakup between him and Sterling Sloane, frontman of The Astral Complex, a less successful but more established emo band. The scathing breakup album Jason's band Synesthesia released less than a year later was the final nail in the coffin for his career; the album sounded great, but the lyrics were pointedly personal and cruel even to casual listeners, much less those who had been following the entire sordid saga.

Both Jason and Sterling had fallen far out of the public eye since the breakup that blew up both of their careers. Parker had interviewed Jason once, but it had been long before Jason started dating Sterling—an eager, starry-eyed twenty-year-old prodigy. The prospect of interviewing him again, knowing how reclusive he'd become, was sorely tempting.

Taylor would be understanding, he was sure. And he could just come by the next day instead. Parker swore under his breath before adding more loudly,

"Yeah, alright. I'll do it. Send me the address."

"That's what I wanted to hear," Tim cawed cheerfully, which only irritated Parker more. But he wasn't doing it for Tim, he told himself—if Jason was working on a new album, maybe he could get him to agree to come onto his podcast to help promote the album later on, and that would be sure to draw plenty of new listeners. The better his podcast did, the sooner he could leave Punk News Net and Tim's annoying voice completely.

He was sure Tim would have taken the interview if he refused, but Tim was the definition of a sellout if there

ever was one. When he'd created the music news site, he'd
been a journalist—just as passionate and curious as Parker
was—but the success of Punk News Net meant he could rest
on his laurels and let the staff do all the hard work. Very
un-punk, but the gig was still too good for Parker to leave.

For now, though, he'd take the stupid interview if just for
the chance to talk one on one with the reclusive singer.

/ /

Parker

> Hey, I have to postpone Friday. I'm really
> sorry, can we do Saturday instead? I hate
> to keep rescheduling but apparently
> Jason Daugherty's agent reached out
> and Tim's creaming his pants over the
> chance to get an interview with him on
> PNN, and no one else can do it.

Taylor

> The Synesthesia Jason Daugherty?
> Damn dude that's pretty cool. Saturday
> still works for me, so no worries. See you
> then and good luck interviewing him. Do
> you think he'd flip if you asked him about
> Sterling?

> **Parker**
> Thanks for being so understanding. And lol probably yeah, I think I'll avoid the topic if I wanna keep my job. Although I would love to be done with Tim and PNN for good. Maybe if I can get Jason on the podcast...

> **Taylor**
> I'm rooting for you dude. Then you can really ask him about Sterling.

> **Parker**
> Lol I'll keep that in my back pocket. See you Saturday then!

//

The interview was up in Los Angeles on a Friday morning, the worst kind of commute. He left his apartment before the sun was up, but by the time he pulled up in front of the address Tim had given him, it was so hot he started sweating as soon as he got out of the car.

The house they were meeting in was almost certainly not Jason's—while it wasn't a mansion by any means, it was still a decent-size house near Silver Lake. An album every few years, and a tour just as infrequently, wouldn't be paying those kinds of bills.

Parker rang the doorbell, and the door swung open almost immediately. A tall woman with long, wavy blonde hair in a tight-fitting black tank top, skinny jeans, and flower tattoos up the length of one arm answered. "Hello."

"Hi, uh, I'm Parker Flores," Parker tried to say with confidence, glancing past her to make sure he was in the right place after all. "With Punk News Net...?"

She nodded, smiling. "Great. I'm Lyssa, Jason's agent. Come on in."

"Thanks," Parker agreed, stepping inside. "I guess you probably talked to my boss Tim, then?"

She laughed as she led him through the entryway, the low heel of her black ankle boots clicking on the tile with every step. "Sure did. He was really eager for the interview. I know Jason's done interviews with PNN before, so I figured it would be a safe bet. Jason, Parker's here."

The living room was a cozy, bohemian sort of space with plenty of light flooding in from the wide windows. Jason sat on a mustard-yellow loveseat, but stood as they entered. He looked better than Parker had been expecting, all things considered: his hair was short, and he had a tidy, full beard. He'd gained some weight since Parker had seen him last, but Parker supposed that finally kicking a drug habit would do that to anyone. He had several tattoos up his arms, and the hint of more ink along his collarbones from the slight flash of exposed skin Parker could see there under his black V-neck. Overall, he looked perfectly normal.

"Hey," Jason said, reaching out his hand. "Shit, I recognize you now. Lyssa told me I'd done an interview with you once before. I didn't remember, but seeing your face—wow, that must have been a decade ago, right?"

Parker laughed, nodding. "Yeah, at least. I might have still been in high school, even. I think it was for a little local zine."

"Small world," Jason laughed, shaking his head. "Well, good to see you again. Thanks for taking the interview."

"Please, sit. Do you want anything to drink?" Lyssa interrupted, gesturing toward the brown sofa across from the loveseat where Jason had been sitting. A glass-topped coffee table stood between them with a candle and some magazines, along with a mug of coffee on the side closest to Jason. On the far side between them, a chair that didn't quite match seemed to have been pulled up too—a plush emerald chair that looked like it should have been in an office rather than a living room.

Lyssa must have noticed him clocking it, as she said quickly, "I'll be sitting in just to make sure he doesn't say anything too out there. I'm sure you understand."

It certainly wouldn't be the first time he'd interviewed someone with their agent present, but it often made for less-interesting interviews. He wondered what Jason might say that worried her—his public reputation wasn't exactly shining already, so there wasn't much that he could do to make things much worse for himself.

"Not a problem," Parker said quickly, shrugging. He sat down and started to set up his recorder on the table between them. "And, yeah, some water would be great, actually."

Lyssa nodded. "I'll bring you some. Be back in a sec."

He could feel Jason watching him as he fiddled with his recorder, then pulled out his tablet to take notes.

"So, uh, Tim didn't have a lot of details as to what you wanted to talk about, just that you're doing a new album?" Parker asked once he had all his equipment ready. Jason chuckled, nodding.

"Yeah, that's the main thing," he said. "Lyssa wanted me to do some interviews to, uh, improve my reputation, in her words. I'm doing a lot better now, actually, but I haven't done any kind of interviews since I was, uh, not doing so well. She's wanting to set the groundwork for a better public reception before we announce the album."

"I hear you talking in there already," Lyssa called from the kitchen.

"Nothing on the record yet," Parker called back with a laugh. Jason rolled his eyes, but remained smiling; still, Parker waited until Lyssa was back in the room to speak again. She handed him a bottle of water—one of the fancy glass bottles that wouldn't make noise when he opened it, which was a point in her favor.

"Alright, so, I've got some questions here we can fall back to, but I figured you'd probably want to take the lead today. Does that sound good?" Parker asked. Jason glanced at Lyssa, who nodded, then he nodded as well. "Great. Just tell me whenever you're ready, and I'll start recording."

Lyssa settled into the green armchair between them, pulling up her phone. "You won't even know I'm here," she whispered.

"I'm ready," Jason said, and Parker nodded, first taking a long drink of water, then hitting the record button.

"So, Jason," he started, leaning back with his tablet. "First, I'm curious as to what you've been up to since your last album release. You're one of the last holdouts against having any sort of personal social media, and the band's socials are pretty much business-only. So I'm sure a lot of fans are wondering how you've been."

"Well, I was definitely going through it," Jason sighed. "But I'm doing a lot better now. Honestly, I'm probably never going to be on any kind of social media—my mental health is already shit enough without it, you know? If I had been live-tweeting my first rehab stint, I probably would be in a very different place right now."

Parker chuckled, glancing over at Lyssa, but she seemed unconcerned with her eyes still on her phone.

"But, yeah, for a while I was in rehab again," Jason continued. "This time I kept it pretty quiet. Knowing everyone knew I was in rehab the first time made it harder for everything to stick, I think. But I'm doing a lot better now. I've been sober over a year now, so I think I'm ready to get back into the swing of albums and touring and all that."

"That's great to hear," Parker said, nodding. "And congrats on a year sober. That's no easy feat. I'm really glad to hear that. So are you working on a new album now? Or is one already in the pipeline?"

"I wrote a lot of songs when I was in rehab, so the album's coming really soon. It's already in the works. And, I mean, I stand by all my work, really; but I think this album is some of my best." Jason paused, his eyes flicking over to Lyssa before he added, "Well, I stand by most of my work. If I could go back in time and change anything... I don't know. I'm not exactly proud of *Dying to Leave* anymore, but it really changed the trajectory of my life forever. It was really hard, but I'm proud of the person I am today, finally, and I don't know how different I would be without that album."

Lyssa's fingers were hovering over her phone, clearly listening intently, but she didn't look up at them or interrupt.

"It's definitely part of the lasting legacy of the band," Parker agreed, watching Lyssa too. "Has it been difficult to move on from that? I know that a lot of critics will always go back to that as the ultimate representation of the band, even over your previous albums that really launched so much of your initial success in the first place."

"It's tough for sure," Jason agreed. "But, I mean, what's done is done. There's no point in wishing I could change the past. It took a long time for me to really accept that. That everything that happened is on me, not Sterling—"

"Nope," Lyssa interrupted, holding up a hand to stop him. "No mentions by name."

"Right, sorry," Jason muttered. "Well, long story short, yeah, it's been challenging. But I'm doing really well right now. Trying to take things one day at a time, but I really feel like this year has been a turning point for me. The first time I went to rehab, I had been spiraling because I hated how *Dying to Leave* was going to define me, and especially the rest of the band. And, I mean, all the shit that led up to that, too. But I spent a lot of time in therapy trying to grapple with that and be grateful for all the success I had. I'm lucky enough to still make music for a living. That's what I'm trying to focus the most on, instead of dwelling on what I used to have, or thought I could have had."

"That's some really good stuff," Parker agreed, glancing between Jason and his notes. "I think that's what it comes down to in the end, being grateful for what we have instead of obsessing over what we think we should have."

"It's all about mindfulness, dude, seriously," Jason laughed. "Wish I wasn't so hard-headed. I feel like a lot of people could have gotten that from a book, but it took me two rounds of rehab and a lot of therapy to really get that. Anyway, uh, that's a lot of what the new album is about. Just trying to reflect on all that."

"Does the album have a name yet?"

"I'm throwing a few ideas around—"

"Just stick with the working title for now," Lyssa interjected. "Parker, we'll contact you if it ends up changing before release. It might change."

Jason visibly scowled. But whatever the story was there, Parker was sure he wasn't going to hear it now. He nodded, then looked back at Jason.

"The title right now is *What Remains*. I feel like it's going to be a total opposite to *Dying to Leave*, so I tried to kind of... reverse the title, I guess. Staying instead of leaving. A lot of it is about trying to learn to be happy with the person you are, instead of finding worth in the person you're with. That kind of shit."

Parker chuckled, nodding. "No, I like that. It's a nice balance between a nod toward it and moving on to the next thing, which it sounds like is a lot of what the album touches on."

They went back and forth about the new album for a while, as Jason went more in-depth on his process of writing much of it in rehab, and how starkly different the recording process felt going at it sober. Luckily, Lyssa didn't interrupt again.

"Alright, I think I've got enough for the article," Parker said when they'd been talking for close to an hour. "Unless there's anything else you want to add?"

"Hold on, sorry," Lyssa said quickly. She stood, but was still looking at her phone. "Ugh, I need to take a call from another client really quick. Sorry, guys. I'll be right back. Nothing on the record while I'm gone, alright?" She shot Parker a sharp look; but her expression softened, and she laughed as she walked away.

"Right," Parker agreed, laughing nervously. Both he and Jason were silent until the click of another door echoed down the hall.

"Well, hey, since we're off the record," Jason said, pulling Parker's attention back to him. "You're friends with the guys from Get Well Soon, right?"

"Oh," Parker said, surprised. That was one of the last things he'd expected from Jason—but Get Well Soon was a pretty big name now, even for someone who wasn't on social media at all. "Uh, yeah. I know them."

"God, what a shame," Jason sighed, shaking his head. "How's everyone doing? Do you know what they plan to do with Zach gone?"

Parker grimaced, unsure of how much he should say. But Jason seemed, if not trustworthy, at least so absent from the media that there was little risk of anything he said now making it to a wider audience.

"I only know a bit," he said carefully. "I'm, uh, mostly friends with Taylor. He's, well... he's doing okay, all things considered. Trying to move on. But, since we're off the record... There's probably never going to be any more music from Get Well Soon, at least not the way it is now."

Jason rubbed one hand over his beard, his eyes tightening in a pained expression. "That's unfortunate to hear. Their stuff was getting better and better. But I can totally understand that. It would never really be the same, anyway."

"Yeah," Parker agreed awkwardly, unsure of what else to say. Jason's hand lingered over his beard; a brighter tattoo on his wrist caught Parker's eye, the crisp lines and bright colors indicative of it being relatively new. It took a moment to recognize it: a braided cord bracelet tattooed over his wrist, bright red with the dangling ends creeping up the back of Jason's hand, blending with another tattoo that was several years older and less distinct.

It instantly brought to mind a lyric from the Astral Complex, Sterling's band—the realization made heat rush into Parker's face, and he glanced away before Jason could notice him staring. He could only half-remember the line, something about being wrapped up in red thread—he'd have to listen to the song on the drive home.

"Well, I'm glad to hear Taylor's doing alright, at least," Jason finally said, shaking Parker from his thoughts. "We met a couple of times in festival circuits mostly. He was always nice when I saw him, though. Sweet guy. Is he like that in real life?"

Parker laughed. "Yeah, he's great. Super sweet." He flushed, hoping Jason wouldn't notice the color rising in his face. They lapsed into silence for a long, awkward moment.

"Sorry, I don't mean to overstep—" Jason started, and Parker shook his head quickly.

"You're not," he blurted out. "We're not—it's not like that. Between us. We're friends."

To his surprise, Jason laughed. "Well, that's not really what I meant. But, you know, if you have to say it…"

Parker was about to burst into flames. Part of him couldn't even understand what Jason was trying to say to him, and the rest of him was hoping he'd fall into a pit to the center of the earth to avoid having this conversation.

Luckily, the door down the hall clicked open before he could think of anything to say in response. He didn't think he would ever have been so grateful to see Lyssa as she reappeared in the doorway, looking down at her phone still with a slightly annoyed expression.

"Sorry about that," she said, clearly oblivious to the awkward silence she'd walked into. "Where were we?"

"I mean, I think we're good," Parker said quickly, gesturing toward Jason without looking at him. "Was there anything else you wanted to make sure we had, Jason?"

Jason was silent for a moment, long enough that Parker risked looking over at him. The man was clearly stifling a smile as their eyes met, amusement obvious in his expression.

"No, I think we're good," he replied simply, though Lyssa now looked suspiciously between the two of them. Parker resolutely shoved his recorder into his backpack.

"What were you talking about while I was gone?" she asked, and Parker couldn't quite tell if her tone was teasing or accusatory. Jason only rolled his eyes.

"Nothing," he said.

"Nothing, huh?" Lyssa repeated.

"My podcast," Parker blurted out, the lie coming easily. "Uh, I have a podcast. I'm not supposed to talk about it when I'm on interviews for PNN, but I was telling Jason that if he ever wants to do another interview when the album comes out..."

Jason shot him a surprised look, but Lyssa only laughed. "Yeah, I saw you had a podcast. Your numbers look pretty good from what I can tell, actually. Some big names here and there too. I'll keep that in mind for next time. And I won't tell Tim. He's kind of a dick anyway."

Parker laughed, probably harder than he should have. "You're telling me."

After a few more formalities and exchanging their goodbyes, Parker headed out. Jason followed him to the front porch, but he only took a hit of a vape he pulled from his pocket, waving goodbye as Parker loaded his things back into his car.

"I'll hit you up about your podcast," he called as Parker got into his car, then he turned for the door again.

When he was safely a few streets away, Parker found the song that Jason's tattoo had reminded him of—it was one of the Astral Complex's early sleeper hits, one that had never been a radio single, off their second album. The line he was thinking of was in the bridge.

Wrists wrapped so tight in our tangled red thread, they'll have to send me down in your coffin, Sterling's plaintive voice cried. *Too scared to go alone, I'd rather die held tight in your bones.*

Chapter Nine
Taylor

Despite how disappointed Taylor had been when Parker had texted him to postpone, knowing it would only be by a day helped soothe the worst of the sting. Taylor was especially curious about how the interview had gone—Jason Daugherty was infamous in their corner of the music world. He'd met the man once or twice, after his scathing breakup album had sent his career into a nosedive. The man seemed nice enough the few times Taylor had met him, but that album cast him in an entirely different light. As far as Taylor knew, this interview with Parker was the first he'd done in at least a year.

Mostly, though, he was looking forward to just being with Parker again; everything felt so much more manageable when they were together. Alone, he started feeling overwhelmed and anxious far too easily, thinking about everything that still needed to be done to get the

Caesura Room fit to actually open. But he and Parker working on it together made it a worthwhile use of his time, something productive to direct his energy into, instead of an endless, fruitless time suck.

The next day, he arrived early to decide what they would work on. The carpet in the upstairs green room would need to be replaced, so he figured they might as well rip it all up—there was more carpet in the box office and the manager's office that was in better shape, but he wanted everything to match, so it all had to go. It would be a difficult task alone, with only one good arm, but the two of them could tackle it much more easily.

The main entrance door swung open, loud enough for Taylor to hear from the green room. A moment later, footsteps echoed on the wood flooring in the pit.

"You here, Taylor?" Parker's voice called, and Taylor stifled a grin.

"Up here!" he called toward the stairs. The sound of Parker's footsteps reverberated through the narrow staircase a moment later, then the man appeared in the doorway, his dark hair tousled. He smiled, and Taylor smiled back—then his eyes flickered down to the graphic t-shirt Parker was wearing, and he laughed.

"Is that an Astral Complex shirt?" Taylor chuckled. The band name was emblazoned across the shirt, the letters thin and golden in an art nouveau style, and a depiction of an astrolabe beneath them. Parker laughed, looking down at the shirt.

"Yeah, I remembered I had this after my interview yesterday," he said, sounding sheepish. "Figured it might give me some street cred."

"Good thing you didn't wear it to the interview," Taylor teased. "How did that go?"

"You know, surprisingly well," Parker replied. "But I can tell you about it while we're working. What are we doing today?"

An hour later they had most of the green room carpet rolled up and set in a pile at the bottom of the stairs, and Taylor had heard all about the surprisingly tame interview with the Synesthesia frontman. He wasn't sure whether to be disappointed it hadn't been juicier, or glad that the troubled man seemed to be doing so well.

"Did you get to hear any of the album he's working on?" Taylor asked, and Parker shook his head.

"No, but I'm hoping he'll do an episode of the podcast when he releases it," he chuckled.

They moved on to the other rooms to rip out the carpet, talking a little more about the interview, then the next interviews Parker had lined up, which somehow led to reminiscing about their college days—when pop-punk had still been cool, and the emo revival was gaining traction.

Parker was quiet after that, which made Taylor nervous as they finished up the last chunk of carpet in the manager's office. When they had rolled it up and placed it with the rest, the other man blurted out,

"So this is really *it* for you, huh?"

Taylor froze, uncertain. "What do you mean?"

Parker gestured around. "All this. The venue. I guess I was just thinking about... I mean, Synesthesia hasn't come out with an album in three or four years now, but Jason's still getting back in the game. It just made me think about you, and the band, and... Well, if you're certain about stepping away from it all."

Taylor looked away, considering it and fiddling with the corner of the ripped-up carpet.

"I don't think I *want* to make music anymore," he finally said. The admission sent guilt pulsing through his chest. "I'm just... over that part of it. But the industry is all I know, and I do still want to be involved in some way... So, yeah, I guess the Caesura Room is *it* for me, if you think of it like that. I like the idea of still being involved in the music world, but just in a different way."

He paused, then chuckled bitterly before adding, "I'm lucky Get Well Soon had gotten so well known. I wouldn't have had the money to get the venue open otherwise. And I don't think I'll have a problem keeping it booked once it does open. So... I'm grateful for everything that made this possible, but I'm ready to move on, you know?"

The words felt more like an admission than Taylor had meant, so he couldn't bring himself to look over at Parker for a long moment. The other man was silent. Finally, Taylor couldn't stand wondering about his reaction anymore and forced himself to look back over at Parker.

He had a small smile on his face, though it wavered when Taylor met his eyes. The way his sweet expression flickered into embarrassment made Taylor's heart skip a beat.

"I get that," Parker said quickly, then chuckled. "I'm glad you feel so sure about it. I know if it were me... I don't know how I'd be keeping all this together. I feel like I'm way too old already to try and get into a new industry, even one that's adjacent like this."

Taylor smirked, glancing away. "Don't say that shit to me, man. We're not that old, not yet."

Parker laughed. His eyes were soft with affection when Taylor looked at him again, and this time the expression lingered for a long moment before Parker turned away again. "Yeah, I guess you're right. Not *yet*."

11

The next two weeks passed in a similar fashion. Parker had committed to one day a week, which typically ended up being when they got the most work done, but Taylor still tried to get into the venue at least once or twice in between to take care of smaller things on his own. He'd called a contractor to take a look at all the sound equipment and a local company to replace all the flooring, both of which came with Zed's recommendation. He was steadily making his way through the list of things that needed to be done before the venue could be opened. In a month or two, he could start thinking about hiring staff, which was daunting.

Luckily, though, he wasn't there yet; and he could spend his days researching everything else that he still needed to do, like all the permits he'd need to apply for to get the venue up and running. His one day each week with Parker was a welcome reprieve from everything clattering around in his head—plus it gave him a much-needed excuse to socialize. Kylie still texted him almost daily, but he hadn't heard from either Dean or Angie since the dinner. Parker and the Caesura Room were really his only reasons for leaving the house.

"Don't forget you have your appointment tomorrow to get your cast off finally," Parker said cheerfully as he walked in on the third week. Taylor laughed.

"Trust me, I remember," he said, holding up his arm. "You're picking me up, yeah?"

"Definitely," Parker agreed. "So what are we working on today?"

Taylor had decided that instead of completely rebuilding the stage, they could replace the few pieces of wood that weren't salvageable, cover up the missing pieces, then strip the remaining wood and refinish the whole thing. Most of it was still in decent shape, he'd found—it was just a few panels that were missing or too damaged to repair. Taylor had deep-cleaned the stage as best he could earlier that week, so they got to work pulling out the bad pieces, then sanding off the varnish on the rest of it—a painstaking process, especially with Taylor's bad arm.

"Maybe I should have hired someone to do this," Taylor groaned. They'd been at it for at least an hour, with not a huge amount of progress to show for it. After a beat, Parker had laughed nervously, then replied,

"It's fine. The longer it takes, the more we get to hang out. Unless you're trying to get rid of me?"

"That's true. I'll keep you around for now," Taylor chuckled, nodding. Parker's nervous smile broadened at his reply, which made his chest tighten with nerves all over again.

They couldn't hear each other well between the masks protecting them from all the sawdust muffling their voices, and the sound of the sander roaring to life, so their conversation had been stilted in the moments when it was turned off. After a long while, Parker looked over at Taylor, who had been sweeping up some of the sawdust, clearly wanting to say something. Taylor paused, looking back at him.

"Do you..." Parker started, sounding nervous. He looked away before continuing, "Do you think you'll ever want to... you know, date someone again?"

For a moment, Taylor couldn't breathe. The question made his chest tighten with longing—but it was a loaded question, too. Why would Parker ask him that if he *wasn't* interested in him? That had to be it, right? He'd hoped so, but this was all but confirmation. Right?

"Sorry," Parker blurted out quickly. Taylor shook himself out of his stupor; he'd been staring silently at Parker for several awkward seconds. "That was really—I shouldn't have asked that. Sorry. God, I couldn't even imagine—forget I asked."

"No, I—I think I will," Taylor interrupted, heart pounding. "I, um, I think I would. I'd like to. Yeah."

They stared at each other for a long moment, and Taylor forced himself to keep meeting Parker's wide eyes.

"I, um," Parker finally stammered. "I'm sorry, anyway. I shouldn't have asked."

"It's okay," Taylor replied, but Parker was already turning the sander back on, his gaze firmly down on the stage. Taylor watched him work for a moment, glad his mask was hiding his small, nervous smile.

That had to be it, right? Parker asked because *he* wanted to date Taylor. Right?

Maybe he should just go for it. Everything he'd wanted to talk to Parker about could wait. He would just go for it.

Their conversation mostly petered out after that, though a few minutes later Parker forcedly asked Taylor about some TV show they'd both been watching, and they talked about that on and off for the rest of the afternoon.

Finally, the stage was largely bare of varnish; they would finish the last of it, replace the missing boards, then re-varnish it the next week. But for now, they were done for the day.

"There are some beers in the fridge," Taylor said, as Parker pulled his mask off. "Want one?"

Parker hesitated, glancing between Taylor and the exit for a moment; but finally, he smiled weakly over at Taylor and nodded. "Yeah, that sounds good. I'm gonna go wash some of this sawdust off my face, then I'll meet you at the bar?"

Taylor nodded, watching as Parker stepped away. His heart was pounding hard in his chest. He could do it. Parker was just as interested. He *would* do it.

Shaking himself into action, Taylor hurried to the small kitchen off to the side of the bar and scrubbed his hands clean in the sink, then opened the back fridge that housed some bottled waters, electrolyte drinks, sodas, and two different six-packs of bottled beers. He'd stocked this fridge for the contractors that were coming in to help repair things. Only two of the beers had been taken, so he grabbed two bottles and popped the caps off. He took a sip of his, focusing on the bitter, hoppy taste to try to ease his sudden nerves.

They didn't have bar stools set up yet, but he still brought both beers over to that side of the bar, setting Parker's bottle on the countertop, before leaning against the bar with his own beer in hand, taking another sip. Was it weird for him to be waiting here? Did he look too casual? Not casual enough?

Luckily, Parker came walking back through the hallway just a moment later, so he didn't have too long to stress over it. His eyes landed on Taylor; he grinned, then took a long drink of his beer, before settling beside Taylor and leaning against the bar.

"That hits the spot," he chuckled, pensively looking down at the beer in his hands. "Thanks, Taylor. I won't tattle that you're serving me beer without an alcohol license."

Taylor laughed. "You didn't buy it, so I don't know if it still counts. But thanks."

"Same time next week, then?" Parker asked, and Taylor nodded. "The stage is gonna look so much better once we're done. Hell, it looks better already."

"It does," Taylor agreed. He looked around the venue for a moment, then shot Parker a small smile. "It's all really coming together, you know? It's finally starting to look like a real, functioning venue. I can actually imagine what it'll look like when everything's done."

Parker's gaze softened, meeting Taylor's eyes. "It's looking great already. You should be really proud of yourself, Taylor."

"I couldn't have done it without you," Taylor replied quickly, feeling the heat rising in his face. "So, you know. Thank you."

"My pleasure," Parker chuckled, then held out his beer toward Taylor. "Here's to the Caesura Room, the next big rock venue in all of San Diego."

Taylor laughed; for an instant, Parker's eyes flickered down to look at his lips when he smiled, then back up at his eyes. "I'll drink to that. Cheers."

They clinked their bottles together, and each took another sip; Taylor's was nearly empty now. They weren't strong drinks by any stretch of the imagination, but it was enough for him to feel the beginnings of a slight buzz—enough that he could trick himself into being brave, he hoped.

He glanced up again. Parker was still watching him. The other man turned away nervously when Taylor caught him looking, but Taylor kept his gaze fixed firmly on Parker, trying to figure out what he was going to say.

"Parker, I..." he stammered. Parker's gaze turned right back to him, his eyes attentive, despite the slight flush rising in his cheeks. "I, um, I really do appreciate this... Everything you've done for me."

His warm brown eyes nearly glowed in the soft light as he smiled back at Taylor. "I'm happy to help."

"I..." Taylor started again, but couldn't find the words. Did he need them? Surely Parker felt it, too? He bit his lip anxiously, and Parker's gaze dropped down to his mouth.

Mustering all his willpower, Taylor leaned forward and kissed him. Parker jolted with surprise, first at the touch of their lips pressing together, then again as Taylor's free hand clasped Parker's forearm. For a moment, the other man was completely motionless—then a faint, broken sound escaped from the back of his throat, and he kissed Taylor back.

Heat erupted across Taylor's skin, centered around the electricity of where their lips met. His heart was still pounding, no longer with anxiety, but from the way each one of his nerves lit up at Parker's responsive touch—the ghost of his rapid, needy breath on Taylor's skin as they kissed. It made him feel like he could do anything. What had he been so afraid of?

But it lasted only a moment. Parker pulled away, taking a full step back and causing Taylor to stumble off-balance as they abruptly parted. His face was flushed, lips glistening in the soft light of the bar, but his eyes were wide and almost fearful. Taylor froze, doubt creeping up the edges of his consciousness all over again.

"Taylor," Parker stammered. "Why—Why—Why did you do that?"

Taylor's mouth worked silently for a moment, trying to find the words that would make Parker's face go back to the sweet, enthralled expression he'd had before.

"Because I—I wanted to," he finally blurted out. "I thought you did, too."

Parker was silent for a long moment, eyes still wide. He didn't deny it, but that only made Taylor feel more unsure of what was happening.

Finally, he croaked out, "We... We shouldn't do this, Taylor."

"But—" Taylor stammered. His heart felt like it might fall out of his stomach. "Why not?"

"This is so wrong," Parker said, finally turning away as he scrubbed an anxious hand through his hair. "I shouldn't... I couldn't do this to you, to Zach. Fuck, I introduced you guys. I shouldn't want you—want this." His face had grown more flushed the longer he spoke, his nervous movement a stark contrast to the steady resolve growing in Taylor's chest.

This was it. He had to tell the truth.

"Zach is gone," he said, his voice coming out hoarse. "He's dead. If we both want this, then that's all that matters."

"It's only been, what, three, four months? This feels way too—*way* too soon, Taylor. I would feel terrible... And if people thought—" Parker protested, still not meeting Taylor's eyes.

"No, it's been more than four months. Zach and I..." Taylor said. Despite everything, he couldn't stop the stab of pain in his chest as he forced the words out. "Zach and I were going to get divorced."

Chapter Ten
Parker

THEN

Parker kept telling himself that he was only nervous because it was a little weird to be driving the cute guy in his poetry class to his friends' parents' house so he could play piano in their garage. Right? The whole situation was kind of funny. So if he felt nervous, that was the only reason.

Taylor seemed a little nervous too, sitting quietly in the passenger seat as they made the drive up to Zach's parents' house. Which was understandable. He was probably worried about whether Zach would let him join the band. Why else would he be nervous?

Parker turned the music up a little louder, hoping that would fill in the awkward silence between them more effectively. At least it wasn't too long of a drive.

When they got off the freeway, Taylor finally looked over at him and said, "So... what's your friend's name again?"

"Oh, uh, his name's Zach," Parker stammered in reply, turning the music back down. "We went to a lot of the same shows in high school, so when we started recognizing each other, we talked and hung out a few times, and found out we were going to the same college. We actually live on the same floor now."

"What's he like?" Taylor continued. Parker considered it for a moment, unsure of the best way to describe Zach.

"He's cool," he finally answered. "He's really friendly and outgoing. And he goes to a ton of shows."

"Do you think he's any good?" Taylor asked, holding back a laugh. Parker chuckled.

"I haven't heard him play guitar," he admitted. "But I think he's a good singer. I mean, I've really only heard him singing along at shows, but I always thought he sounded pretty good. So I don't think the band will be a *total* flop, if that's what you're worried about."

He could see Taylor smiling in amusement out of the corner of his eye, and he hoped his face hadn't turned as red as it felt.

When they pulled up to the house, the garage door was open, and Parker could see everyone was already there. The drum kit stood in the corner with one of Zach's friends sitting behind it, and he could see two more figures—they looked like girls—sitting on a sofa that was pushed up along the other side of the garage. Zach himself was standing in front of the drum set, talking to the drummer.

"Are they all trying out for the band, too?" Taylor asked, sounding a little dismayed as they parked.

"I don't think so," Parker replied quickly. "That's the guitarist and the bassist. I think it's just someone on keyboard they were still looking for."

They got out of the car. Zach had turned toward them with a wide smile on his face.

Parker was about to barf. Zach wasn't really his type, so he hadn't considered it, but Zach was *hot*—and he was about to introduce him to the guy he had a crush on. Maybe his long dark hair, and his snakebite piercings, and his toned, tattooed arms *were* Taylor's type—not at all like Parker's tidy haircut and his skinny, unathletic frame.

"Hey!" Zach called as they walked up the driveway. "Good to see you, Parker. Is this your friend?"

"Yeah," Parker stammered, looking back at Taylor. "This is the guy I was telling you about, Taylor. Taylor, this is Zach."

To his dismay, Parker could see how Zach's eyes flickered up and down Taylor's frame, lingering for just a beat before he held out his hand. "Nice to meet you. I'm Zach. Parker was telling me you're a music major?"

Taylor's cheeks had taken on a pinkish flush, and he pushed his hair back from his face nervously with one hand, as the other returned the handshake.

"Yeah," he said breathlessly. "I've only ever done, like, classical stuff, but I've always wanted to be in a rock band. So when Parker said you were looking, I thought it sounded perfect."

Zach's eyes softened with a smile. "Sounds perfect to me. C'mon, I'll introduce you to everyone, and then we can play a couple songs and see how you vibe with us."

Parker looked away, nausea rising in his gut. Whatever chance he might have had with Taylor was gone forever; it was obvious just from the way they looked at each other. Taylor had never looked at him with such a sweetly flustered expression, and he'd never seen Zach with so much heat in his eyes. If Taylor was an angel, then Parker was just a plain old human, and Zach was a fucking god. Maybe he'd never really had a chance in the first place.

"Hey, Parker!" one of the girls called, waving as she stood up from the sofa where the other girl still sat. Her voice snapped Parker out of his spiral of hurt feelings, and he forced a smile back as he waved. She was tall and blonde with a septum ring, and he recognized her from a few of the shows he and Zach had gone to together in the past.

"Hey, Kylie," he replied, remembering her name just in time. "How are you?"

They chatted briefly, but Parker could barely focus on anything she said. Zach got Taylor set up with the keyboard that they had in the corner, then Parker flopped down miserably onto the sofa.

"Parker, wanna jam with us?" Zach called from where he was still standing beside Taylor at the keyboard. Parker waved the suggestion away with a forced laugh.

"Trust me, you don't want to hear me sing," he replied, but he couldn't bring himself to look at either of them, hoping he didn't appear as miserable as he felt.

What the hell had he been thinking, bringing Taylor here? He never should have told him about stupid Zach and his stupid band. The thought was silly and juvenile, but no one else was paying attention to him as the band started playing, so he could safely sulk for now. It was too late to do anything else, anyway.

11

Now

For a moment, the whole world froze. Parker couldn't move—couldn't tear his eyes away from the scuffed spot on the floor where he'd fixed his gaze to avoid looking at Taylor's betrayed expression. What was he saying? That couldn't possibly be true, could it?

"W-What?" he finally stammered, barely able to hear his own voice over the pounding of his heart. "No. No, you weren't. There's no way."

"We *were*," Taylor insisted, and the utter anguish in his voice forced Parker to finally tear his eyes away from the floor to look back at the other man. His blue eyes, so full of warmth and hope just a few moments ago, were now guarded and cold. "I... I know how it sounds, bringing it up now, but we were waiting until after the tour to... to make it public, and then—and then everything happened, and I..."

Taylor turned away abruptly, shaking his head. "So it's not... It's not like that, Parker, okay? That shouldn't factor into this between us. Please."

As much as he trusted Taylor, part of Parker still couldn't quite believe it. Zach and Taylor had been perfect for each other. They were *the* gay power couple of the music world: college sweethearts who had made it through the slog of being small-time touring musicians into the wild success Get Well Soon had finally achieved, like a modern fairy tale.

Had it all been a lie, a front? Parker couldn't wrap his head around it.

"I—I don't know what to say," he managed to stutter after a long, uncomfortable moment of meeting Taylor's expectant gaze. "I think... I need to think about this, Taylor. This is a lot."

Taylor had gone very still, his eyes still downcast. He was silent for a beat, then he took in a long, shaking breath.

"Okay," he said, his voice faint. "Sorry. You don't have to stay. I'll close everything up."

He wanted to protest, to try to talk things out, to think things through; but he couldn't seem to coordinate any of his thoughts into coherent words.

"Taylor," he managed to get out. "Hold on, I mean—"

"Go," Taylor interrupted—it wasn't quite a snarl, but there was a hardness underlying his tone that hadn't been there before. He faced away from Parker now, turned toward the door to the kitchen with his arms folded tightly in front of him, head downturned. "Just... Go home, Parker."

Parker stared at him for a long moment, trying to come up with something, *anything*, to justify staying; but his mind was still blank. Taylor kept his back turned to him as Parker slowly stepped away from the bar, turned toward the exit, and walked through the hallway to the front door. It rattled behind him, then he was alone on the street.

The air bit his skin with cold, but the streets bustled with activity—downtown on a Saturday evening meant all the nearby restaurants and bars were full of life and activity, their light and noise spilling out onto the sidewalk.

But the Caesura Room behind him was dark and silent. Parker took one step, then another, until he'd walked mechanically all the way back to where he'd parked. He drove home in silence, Taylor's words still rattling around in his mind. By the time he'd arrived back at his apartment, he still couldn't make sense of it all.

/ /

Some things became clear the next morning, after Parker had slept on it, but so much of the last night's revelations remained a complete mystery to him.

Taylor and Zach hadn't been together when Zach died. Somehow, it felt like a betrayal, which Parker knew made no sense; but some part of him couldn't get over the idea that they had been planning this for a year and never told him. They weren't as tight knit as they'd been back in college, sure, but Parker still considered both of them friends, especially Taylor—and he'd been the one who introduced them, if nothing else. Somehow, that only created an extra layer to it all, adding a strange sense of personal failure and guilt to all his confusion.

Why were they separating? Had something happened between them? There was surely more Parker didn't know, more Taylor hadn't told him.

But the band must have known, and he would bet money that was why Dean had been so weird to him at Taylor's house—they had all been weird, honestly, but Dean had acted the most outwardly hostile. He must have thought Parker knew, too, and was... what? Trying to make his move on Taylor? If he'd known Zach and Taylor had been separated for so long, though, then why did he care?

There had to be more to the story.

He still couldn't make heads or tails of why Taylor would have waited so long to tell him now. Wanting to keep a separation under wraps until their summer tour was over, he could understand—but Taylor could have told *him* at any point in the months that Parker had been helping Taylor out, bringing him food, checking in on him, making sure he got out of the house... He'd thought Taylor had been grieving his husband, but maybe for Taylor it had been for something else entirely.

Underneath all of it, though, was the heat still simmering deep in Parker's chest: Taylor had kissed him, *wanted* him, and for too short of a moment, he'd kissed Taylor back. The other man hadn't been wrong in his assertion. He *did* want Taylor. He'd just been so caught off-guard at the realization that his feelings were reciprocated after all that he hadn't been able to articulate any of his thoughts, not in any meaningful way, at least.

He blew it—*again*—but hopefully this time he hadn't completely fumbled his shot.

Maybe they would be able to talk about it after Taylor got his cast off. He hadn't heard anything from the other man, so tentatively assumed that they were still good for Parker to take him to the appointment. Now, at least, he could put some of his thoughts into words. His chest still ached with guilt and confusion—wanting Taylor, yet feeling it was somehow wrong of him—but maybe if they could talk things out, it would all start making more sense.

A few hours before he and Taylor had planned to meet, he texted the other man:

Parker

> Still on for your appointment today, yeah?

But Taylor didn't respond. He could see Taylor had read the text when he checked it a little while later, but there was no reply. It made Parker unsettled, but he decided he would still go pick Taylor up. He needed to get his cast off, finally, regardless of... what had happened between them last night. He wasn't so petty that he'd go back on his word to Taylor now.

So later that afternoon he headed out, driving to Taylor's house despite the lack of response to his text. Taylor hadn't told him *not* to come, he argued with himself in the car, so going was the right thing to do.

Parker

I'm here

He texted Taylor again, once he'd parked outside the other man's house. Again, after a moment, the read receipt appeared under the message, but still no response from Taylor came.

Parker huffed half in frustration and half in worry, checking his phone every few minutes as he sat and waited, but Taylor never replied. Finally, Parker got out of his car and walked up to the front door.

He stood there for a moment, feeling awkward and exposed, until he finally forced himself to knock on the door.

"Taylor?" he called, peering around to see if any of the windows were open—he couldn't tell from here. "Are you home?"

He hadn't really expected a response, but the anxiety in his gut only increased the longer he stood there. He tried calling Taylor now, instead of texting him; the phone rang three times, then went to voicemail. Parker hung up without leaving a message, sighing and scrubbing a hand through his dark hair.

He didn't want to be presumptuous enough to check the door; and even if it was unlocked, it would feel too weird to just waltz into Taylor's home uninvited. Something told him Taylor didn't want to see him at all right now, but he didn't want to just let Taylor miss the doctor appointment, either.

He knocked again to no answer, then in frustration sent another text.

Parker

> Please just let me know you're alive.

This time, when the read receipt appeared under the text, the little gray box popped up showing that Taylor was typing, which allowed him to breathe a sigh of relief.

Taylor

> I'm fine. I don't feel well so I'm skipping the appointment. I'll go some other time.

The message's tone was clipped, and Parker was sure Taylor wasn't sick, but upset with him and didn't want to see him—he felt nauseous with worry. If he had been better at hiding his feelings about Taylor, they wouldn't be in this situation at all.

With a sigh, Parker turned and walked back to his car. What else could he do? He hesitated behind the wheel for a moment, wondering if he should go back over to the door and keep knocking, to make sure Taylor went to his appointment, or at the very least get the other man to acknowledge him so they could talk about things.

But the last thing he wanted was to come across as aggressive and pushy, no matter how frustrated it made him feel. So, with a resigned sigh, he turned the car on and drove back home.

11

For the next few days, it was radio silence. Parker tried to keep busy as much as he could—which wasn't too difficult, with several interviews lined up for the week, plus his usual article for the site. Still, through everything, he kept thinking about Taylor and their last conversation. What had happened with him and Zach? And what did that mean about him and Taylor? He kept going back to the moment Taylor had kissed him, replaying the instant their lips pressed together over and over in his head. Every time, the thought made his face flush with warmth.

He wanted to talk about it. He wanted to know what Taylor had been thinking, what he had hoped would happen, what it meant for them going forward—but he couldn't convince himself to try reaching out to Taylor first.

After three days, though, he couldn't stand the unknown anymore and finally texted Taylor.

Parker

> Hey, just want to make sure you're still alright. Can we talk when you get the chance?

He didn't expect a reply, but to his surprise, the read receipt appeared under the message almost immediately. The little typing icon appeared, then vanished—appeared, then vanished again. He watched it intently, wondering what Taylor was typing, wondering how much of it the other man would actually send.

Taylor

> I'm ok. There's nothing to talk about.

Parker stared at the text for a long while, frowning down at his phone. He couldn't bring himself to be mad at Taylor, not really, but this sparked some frustration. Nothing to talk about? It felt like they had *everything* to talk about. He could understand Taylor withdrawing, but this?

Parker

> I really want to talk about this. I want to see you. Please. Can we meet up sometime this week?

This time, while the message was read quickly, no reply came. He stared at his phone until the screen turned off automatically, then put it away with a frustrated groan.

Part of him wanted to go to Taylor's house right then and pound on the door until the other man had to let him in. But how much good would that do? If Taylor didn't want to talk to him, going to his house would only make things worse.

Taylor texted him while he was moping, so he didn't see it right away.

Taylor

> It's fine. I'll see you for the usual on Friday. Talk then if you want.

He couldn't tell if the words made him relieved or more upset. Friday was still days away; he wasn't sure if he could sit quietly with the same churning guilt and confusion and *longing* until then.

God, why had he ever introduced them? Why hadn't he just told Taylor how he'd felt back then, before Zach had come and swept him off his feet? None of this would have ever happened if he could have been honest from the start. He regretted it often, but somehow it burned worse than ever now that he knew what Taylor's mouth felt like pressed against his own.

But it was stupid to think about those kinds of what-ifs. He'd been a college kid with a crush, still insecure in his sexuality—a relationship with Taylor back then would have been nothing like a potential relationship with him now.

And they did have that potential now. Maybe. It would depend on how things went on Friday.

With a resigned sigh, he typed out a few different responses before finally just sending back:

Parker

Ok. See you then.

Chapter Eleven
Taylor

He never should have said anything.

The thought must have echoed in Taylor's mind at least a thousand times after their disastrous kiss. He had been so confident, so *sure* that Parker had wanted him back—but he had been wrong. He'd even finally admitted the truth that had been gnawing at his insides for months, and somehow that had made things worse.

He didn't understand it, but he regretted ever offering a drink to Parker that night. Why hadn't he just said goodnight and let the other man go home, the way he had every other time they'd worked on the Caesura Room together?

He had been afraid Parker would still turn up for his appointment; and sure enough, Parker texted him, called him, even came knocking at his door. But Taylor had been completely immobilized with... he wasn't quite sure what.

A bitter mix of embarrassment and regret and a grief that cut to the bone—completely different from the deep muscle ache of mourning for Zach and everything that had happened between them. No, this was sharp and acrid bile that he couldn't swallow down.

He barely got out of bed for days. He should have had his cast off—had planned to do some work around the venue that the cast had proved too unwieldy to work around—but instead he curled up under his blankets, listened to music, and watched TV. One day, maybe, he might be able to someday face Parker again without wanting to be swallowed up into the center of the earth.

Then Parker texted him again, begging to talk, and Taylor's heart tumbled right out of his chest. *Why?* Why did Parker string him along like this? What more was there to tell? There was nothing that could take back what had happened, so why did it matter?

And that small, stupid, pathetic part of him he'd never been able to tamp down was so starved for Parker's attention that he could barely muster a deflection until Friday, when they'd planned to meet, anyway. Now that he knew his feelings weren't reciprocated, why did he still want to be around the other man? And why did Parker want to be around him now, pathetic as he was, knowing that Taylor wanted him that way? Did he get off on seeing Taylor pining after him? He didn't think that was the case; but even if it was, it somehow didn't bother Taylor enough to cut him out of his life forever. No, they still planned on meeting on Friday.

What the hell was wrong with him? He didn't *like* suffering this way, so why was he still so drawn to Parker, so eager to see him again? It made him feel like an idiot, but he still couldn't say no when Parker asked if they were still on for Friday.

So, miserably, he dragged himself out of bed. Once he showered, and washed his hair, and shaved his face, he did a load of laundry and ate something that wasn't takeout. The stupid cast still on his arm meant everything took twice as long to do. He thought about calling the clinic himself to schedule a new appointment, but froze with fear every time he pulled the number up. No, getting himself presentable was about all he could manage for now.

When Zach had died, one of the first things Taylor had done was take down all the pictures on the walls. A lot of the pictures of them together had been taken down long before, when they had first decided to part ways, but a few still remained—family photos, mostly, and an occasional photo of one or the other alone. Taylor packed them away a few days after the funeral, hating how much it made the house feel haunted, like Zach was still there somehow, watching him.

The feeling came creeping back now, as he painstakingly folded laundry in the living room, even though there were no pictures on the walls. This had been their house, Zach's house, and the memory of him still lingered in every corner. Taylor scowled, keeping his eyes down at the pile of laundry—if he looked up, he would certainly catch sight of Zach's ghost staring at him from across the room. He wasn't sure if Zach would be laughing at him, or looking at him with pity; he wasn't sure what would be worse.

Somehow, this would be so much less complicated if Zach was still alive. They would have been actually divorced by now, not just talking about it—if not now, then soon—and whatever he had going on with Parker might have felt weird in a different way, but it wouldn't have been like *this*.

But Zach was gone. His ghost wasn't there; if there *was* a ghost, Taylor was sure Zach wouldn't be haunting *him*. So he kept his eyes downturned, ignoring that feeling of being watched as he worked.

When he finally raised his head to bring his laundry up the stairs, the walls were just as bare, the room just as empty.

//

Taylor left his house early the next day, far earlier than usual to meet Parker, but he wanted some time in the Caesura Room to himself. He hadn't so much as thought about the venue since their last meeting and wanted to look things over before deciding what they would do together—the more he could get done on his own, the less time he had to spend with Parker. It should have been a relief, but his stomach twisted in knots.

The stage still needed to be finished. He'd scheduled a contractor to come in and replace the carpets and the wood floors, as well as a repairman to fix various small things in the kitchen, mostly tuning up the appliances. The only things left for him and Parker were odd jobs here and there, before repainting the walls and doing one last deep clean once everything was fixed. The air and heat worked, and he had the forms filled out for the liquor permit... After that he could focus on staffing and then finally opening the venue. It was coming together so much faster than he'd anticipated.

Because of Parker. He would always think of Parker now when he was in the venue; his handiwork was all over it. The realization should have turned his stomach, but he couldn't truly bring himself to be upset about it. Maybe he *did* like suffering.

Taylor set to work slowly sweeping the main floor; it still had some debris and sawdust from their earlier work on the stage. He'd only just finished when he heard the front door rattle open, and he froze, grip tightening over the broom in his one good hand.

Parker appeared in the entryway, his steps coming to a stop as his eyes landed on Taylor across the room. Normally so put-together, now he looked almost as disheveled as Taylor felt, his hair messy and his facial hair scruffy. Something in his expression was hungry, *starving,* and the whole world froze around them.

Even in those few seconds, something about being with Parker, seeing him, made everything Taylor thought he knew turn on its head. His understanding of what had happened between them, which had made so much sense when he was alone, was entirely wrong. The things he couldn't comprehend on his own now inexplicably clicked into place.

Parker's expression was so blatantly full of *want* that Taylor couldn't believe he'd truly thought Parker wasn't interested in him. Sure, he had freaked out, but maybe that was understandable, all things considered. He was scared—more scared than Taylor was—about what this all meant for their relationship. Of course he hadn't been acting rationally—neither had Taylor.

He wanted to kick himself. Why did he get so in his head about this? Why hadn't he just listened when Parker tried to talk to him?

"Um," Parker finally stammered, color rising in his cheeks. Taylor shook himself out of his stupor, wondering how long they'd stood there staring at each other in silence. "Hi."

Despite himself, Taylor's mouth twitched into a small smile. "Hey," he said, looking away self-consciously. "Uh, thanks for coming."

Parker was silent for a long moment; then he took a slow, cautious step further into the room, as Taylor busied himself with putting the broom away. "Yeah, no problem. So, uh... What are we working on today?"

From the cover of the broom closet, Taylor scrubbed an anxious hand over his face, then turned back to face Parker again. "Let's get those last baseboards on the stage, and then we can put the new varnish on."

Parker nodded. Taylor's eyes landed on him again, and he responded with a slow, hesitant smile. "Alright, sounds good. I'll get started."

Taylor helped him gather up the pieces of wood along with the drill and other equipment he'd need, then went to prep everything for the new varnish as Parker set to work. They worked silently for a while, the sound of the electric drill the only noise between them as Parker installed the boards, and Taylor painted the varnish on the opposite end of the stage. Taylor tried to focus on what he was doing, but his thoughts were a jumbled mess. What was he going to say to Parker? What *should* he say? Did Parker even want to talk to him now? Was it already too late?

Parker made quick work of the few panels that needed to be replaced, then carefully swept up his side of the stage before grabbing an extra brush and painting on the varnish. Between the two of them, they put the first coat on quickly, and soon they were standing awkwardly off to the side to let it dry—neither moving to do anything else, but not quite looking at the other, either.

It was Parker who finally broke the silence. "So, uh... How are you holding up?"

Taylor held back a laugh and shrugged, eyes still self-consciously avoiding Parker. "I've been better for sure. But I guess I'm feeling alright today."

"Good," Parker replied, sounding genuinely relieved. After a beat, he added, "I, um, I really missed talking to you this week."

This time, Taylor couldn't stifle his smile, his heart stuttering in his chest. "Yeah... Me too. Sorry. I don't... I don't know what to say, except that I freaked out. Sorry."

"I'm sorry I freaked out, too," Parker replied softly. "I, uh... I don't really know what to think about... everything. But I want you to know I care about you, Taylor. And I don't want to lose you."

They were both silent for a long while, Taylor's heart pounding in his chest so hard that he was sure Parker must be able to hear it. When he finally managed to turn his gaze, the other man's face was tense as he looked down at his feet, but Parker's eyes flickered up to meet his own. He smiled shakily for just a moment, then offered slowly, "Can we talk about it?"

Taylor's expression faltered, and he looked away again. This was what he wanted, wasn't it? So why did he feel so afraid?

"Yeah," he said quickly, before he could talk himself out of it. "Let's go sit in the green room. The new couch is up there."

"That sounds good," Parker agreed, smiling gratefully, before following Taylor up the narrow stairs into the green room. The room looked significantly better than it had when they'd started. He planned on painting the walls a light, cool gray; but some of the decor was already in the room, including the new velvety, dark blue couch that had arrived well over a week ago. He could see the final room clearly in his mind's eye, but he wouldn't be able to bring that vision to life until all the bigger projects were done.

Taylor sat down heavily on the couch. Parker looked down at him for a beat, then carefully sat down on the opposite end of it, several inches of space intentionally kept between them.

"So," Parker said slowly. "I, uh... I have a lot of questions. But maybe you can just... tell me what you want to tell me, then I can ask after."

Taylor gulped down the anxiety rising in the back of his throat. "Yeah. Okay."

Chapter Twelve
Parker

Taylor was silent for a long moment, visibly gathering his thoughts. He ran his hand along the arm of the blue velvet couch, back and forth, leaving a pale mark on the soft fabric where his long fingers brushed across it.

Parker watched him, forcing himself to be patient in spite of the anxiety roiling in his chest. Part of him hadn't really believed Taylor would agree to talk with him about what had happened; the fact that he'd wanted to meet today at all had been a shock on its own. Despite all the questions he wanted to ask, he had to hold it in for now—hopefully, everything Taylor wanted to say would give him answers.

"Zach and I were getting a divorce," Taylor finally said, the words coming out all in a rush. His voice echoed faintly in the mostly empty green room. "About a year ago we had a talk... I was ready to settle down and stop touring. I was just... tired, I guess. Tired of always being somewhere other than home. So I wanted to stop, or at least cut back a lot."

He paused, scrubbing a nervous hand through his hair. His eyes darted toward Parker, but flickered away again just as fast before he continued, "But Zach didn't want to stop. That was where it started. The more we talked about it, the more we knew we were just drifting apart. Nothing bad happened between us, you know? We just wanted different things—things we couldn't have together."

Parker nodded. That part, at least, made some sense to him. Zach had spent all his life chasing the fame and success that they were finally achieving. For him, he was probably seeing things as finally ramping up, and stopping now would be a waste of all the effort that came before. But Taylor was far more laid-back and ready to be done with the grind.

"I wasn't even sure if I wanted to be part of the band anymore, even if we did slow down touring, to be honest," Taylor sighed, looking away. "I don't know. I told Zach that even just fewer tours would be better, but... Now I think I was just trying to hold on to how things were as much as I could. But I was ready to be done even then. And Zach was the frontman, so as long as he wanted to keep going, Get Well Soon would still be around. And we decided that... Well, we had just grown apart, and our relationship wouldn't survive me leaving the band. The summer tour was supposed to be my last, and then we would..."

Taylor paused, clearing his throat. He looked so small and sad curled around himself on the sofa; Parker's chest ached with a mix of sympathy and guilt and frustration all at once. He still had a hundred questions competing to be the first out of his mouth, but he kept silent for now. Interrupting would only slow things down, and he needed to know *everything.*

"Then we would make it official, and I would leave. So that was that," Taylor continued. His eyes remained downturned, arms folded across his chest. "And then Zach started dating someone, and I... I was surprised at how it didn't even hurt. I was even happy for him. I guess we had both been pretty checked out for a while, but with how busy we were all the time, it just didn't feel like it, you know?"

Zach dating someone else so easily, and Taylor not caring, shocked Parker all over again—but clearly his impression of their relationship had been wrong. So instead, he just nodded, watching Taylor attentively as the other man ran a hand through his hair nervously.

Wait. Maybe it was... He blurted out, "It's not Dean, is it?"

Taylor's head swung around to stare at him blankly. "Huh?"

"Who Zach was dating," Parker said, though it was making less sense now that he'd said it. Still, it might explain some of why Dean had been so weird to him at the dinner all those weeks ago. "Is that why he was, like, mad at me or whatever?"

Taylor chuckled and shook his head, allowing Parker to breathe a sigh of relief. "No, it's not Dean, but, uh, actually, it was a friend of Dean's. He got really defensive over how the, uh, some of the money was divided up after Zach passed, so... Me and Angie are good, but I think Dean is still kind of mad at me for his friend, and maybe thought... I don't know."

"Thought what?" Parker asked, still confused.

"I think he thought maybe we were already dating, and you were... benefiting from money he thought should have gone to Rogelio," Taylor said, grimacing. Parker flushed with embarrassment, glancing away. He supposed it was a fair assumption, all things considered. Still, even though he didn't know Dean that well, he couldn't help but wish the other man had just said something so they could all clear the air, instead of shooting him dirty looks in silence.

"And that's why he was being so weird at the dinner," Taylor continued. "But they hadn't been dating very long, and Zach's will still named me the beneficiary, so... Ugh, it was a whole thing. But it's fine. He didn't even ask for anything, but I wanted to—I ended up giving him some money separately, so me and Rogelio are fine, but Dean was still... weird about it for some reason."

Parker wracked his brain trying to think if he knew this mysterious Rogelio, but couldn't think of anyone. Considering his own line of work, though, Parker was sure he knew a thousand people or more who he'd only ever met once and couldn't put a name to if his life depended on it, so maybe they had indeed crossed paths at some point. "Have I met him? Rogelio?"

Taylor shook his head. "I don't think so. I'd only met him a few times before he and Zach started seeing each other. He actually came with us for a few stops on tour before... Before everything happened. I'm glad he wasn't there that night, to be honest. He's a nice guy and all, but..."

He trailed off uncertainly, and Parker shook his head. "You don't have to explain. I get it."

He didn't completely get it, of course, but he could empathize. It would have been an extra, complicated layer of what had already been a horrible situation.

Taylor nodded, still looking uncomfortable, and for a long while, they sat in silence. Taylor stared down at his shoes as Parker watched him, his mind racing. What was the right thing to say? Should he say anything at all?

Eventually, he couldn't hold back the question that had been rattling around in his head the whole time, and asked, "Why didn't you just tell me this sooner, Taylor?"

Taylor flinched, his posture shifting miserably. His legs were crossed tightly in front of him and he rubbed his upper arm self-consciously. Parker hated that the question seemed to pain him so visibly, but it hurt him too—hadn't he deserved to know this, at the very least *before* Taylor had kissed him?

"I just... I was so used to keeping it a secret," Taylor finally rasped out, his voice trembling. "And then Zach was gone, and I didn't want to... It sounds so stupid to say it, but it felt like if I told anyone this after he was gone, I would be tarnishing his reputation or something. Like, why would I tell people we were about to get a divorce when he's dead, you know? What purpose does it serve? It just feels so petty and mean. It's like—"

His voice broke, and he sucked in a shuddering breath, tears glistening on his eyelashes. Parker's chest ached—he wanted to reach out and hug him, wanted to find the right thing to say to comfort him, but couldn't find the words.

"It's like I finally got everything I wanted, but in the opposite way I wanted it," Taylor said, voice still quivering. "No more tours, no more band... And how shitty would I look moving on so fast when my husband just died? And I feel so—I feel so fucking *guilty*."

He shook his head, pressing his hands to his eyes as he tried to stifle his tears—he yanked his right hand away quickly when the hard cast touched his face, and instead scrubbed both eyes with the back of his left hand. Parker could feel his eyes burning too, tears of sympathy and guilt of his own brimming in his vision. He reached across the space between them to place his hand on Taylor's shoulder, unsure of how much more he should comfort him. Taylor leaned into the contact, though, so at least it wasn't entirely unwelcome.

"Parker," Taylor finally croaked—to Parker's surprise, he was half-laughing as he said it. "I've had a crush on you on and off for *years*. I was really hoping that after it was official, I could—I could properly ask you on a date or something, if you weren't seeing anyone. And then all this shit happened, and I... I don't know. I don't know what I'm supposed to do now."

Parker let out a faint, choked laugh, too, the irony of it equal parts painful and comedic. "I had a crush on you the moment I met you, Taylor. I felt so guilty, still feeling that way about you after I introduced you and Zach, but... God, I always regretted it. I wish I had asked you out before you guys ever met. And I—I still feel that way."

He'd held the words in for so long that it almost felt like it was someone else speaking them, not him. But once the admission was out in the open, his heart skipped a beat; his chest was suddenly light, as if he hadn't even realized the weight of what he'd been holding on to for all these years. Taylor turned his head to look over at him, eyes bright with tears. "Yeah? Really?"

Parker nodded, rubbing his eyes with his free hand. "Really."

Taylor let out a sound that was half a laugh and half a cry, rubbing his eyes. Parker looked away, shaking his head miserably. They had been two stupid ships in the night for so long. If he had just said something, anything, at any point, maybe things would be different now.

"So now what?" Taylor's voice was small and quivering. Parker hesitated, unsure of how to respond.

What was the right thing to do? Even if Taylor and Zach had been broken up before Zach passed away, they had still been together for the better part of a decade. Taylor had still just lost his husband a few months ago, even if he had been a soon-to-be ex-husband. It still felt too soon. It would be scummy of him to pursue someone who'd just lost their partner. How could he do that to Taylor, to Zach, when they had both been his friends?

He wanted Taylor—and Taylor wanted him, too. But he had to think about what would be best for Taylor, for both of them—not what was best for his dick, or even his aching heart.

And waiting would be best. Wouldn't it?

"I... I still think maybe we should slow down," he finally gritted out. "I think being in a relationship right now is maybe... not a good idea yet, you know? Not when everything is still so fresh. We should both have a solid understanding of what we want."

Taylor was motionless while Parker spoke, his eyes still downturned. He was silent, so Parker added,

"I just don't want this to be a... a rebound, you know? I know it's been longer for you, but I..."

He trailed off, unsure how to put into words the icy fear that gripped him at the idea of pursuing this with Taylor only for it to end badly. It felt too vulnerable to say out loud, even with everything else they'd discussed so far.

"Yeah," Taylor finally said. "Okay."

He stood abruptly, startling Parker. His voice had been suddenly cool, no longer wavering with emotion. Parker's brows furrowed as Taylor took a step away, rubbing his cast absent-mindedly.

"Taylor," Parker started, unsure of what else to say. Clearly, what he'd said hadn't been what Taylor wanted to hear, but... "I just don't want to get this wrong. It's not that I—"

"I know," Taylor interrupted, then let out a small, strangled-sounding chuckle. "I—I know, Parker. It's fine. I, uh... Let's just finish up the stuff for today, and we can talk about this later, I guess."

Parker wanted to say more, but Taylor was already walking away, heading for the narrow staircase. He couldn't manage to get anything out before Taylor had disappeared down the stairs, leaving Parker alone in the green room. He sighed, scrubbing a hand through his hair in frustration. As much as he'd tried to go into the day without expectations, somehow this still felt like a setback, especially after the conversation they'd just had.

But he really did think it was best to take things slow. Wasn't it? Surely Taylor wanted the same thing as him—to proceed with as little risk as possible to the friendship they already had. He'd even said he didn't want to paint Zach in a bad light after his death, so waiting before jumping into a relationship only made sense, too.

Clearly, though, he was missing a piece of the puzzle—not that Taylor seemed keen on telling him what it was. So with a sigh, he pushed the thoughts away, before standing to follow Taylor down the stairs. He had a job to do, and if he kept busy, he wouldn't dwell on the unsatisfying conclusion to their conversation.

Chapter Thirteen
Taylor

There was something wrong with him. There had to be. That had to be it—that had to be the reason why, after everything, Parker still rejected him.

Everything in Taylor's body had become numb the moment Parker started talking about *taking it slow* and *stepping back*—it was all just a nice way of turning Taylor down. Again. Last time, it felt like shame would set him on fire; now, though, cold seeped from his heart through all his extremities, like all the will and warmth had finally been sapped out of him.

The rest of the afternoon went by in a blur—he wasn't even sure if he and Parker spoke at all after their conversation in the green room—and then he went home, where he immediately stripped naked and stood in the shower. Hot water streamed over him, but he still shivered with cold. He put his face directly in the spray until his hair was soaked, and he almost couldn't breathe.

It didn't help.

Taylor choked, turning his face away from the hot water. Half-coughing, half-sobbing, he pushed his wet hair out of his face and pressed his back to the wall of the shower, sinking down until he was sitting in the tub with his knees pulled up to his chest, water splashing on—

His *cast*.

"Fuck!" he cried, yanking his arm out of the way of the water. It had become such a habit that he just held his right hand above his head whenever he showered, but now he hadn't been as careful. It wasn't too bad—it hadn't been directly under the water for more than a few seconds—and he stumbled out to dry it off quickly. Still, it only made him feel more stupid, more worthless.

He couldn't do anything right. He hadn't been able to keep Zach with him. He hadn't been able to convince Parker to be with him. He couldn't even manage to get the damn cast off his arm that had probably been healed as long as it'd been broken by this point.

When his cast was dry, he ended up sobbing in a heap of towels on the bathroom floor, the shower still running. He wasn't sure how long he spent there.

Had he cried this hard for Zach? Had he been this miserable when they decided to split? When had he fallen out of love with the other man, that parting ways didn't hurt nearly as bad as being rejected by Parker?

He didn't even have the band anymore. All that was left was him. And the Caesura Room.

/ /

Taylor stayed in bed all the next day, ignoring the texts that he got from Parker and Kylie and everyone else. He didn't want to deal with any of it. He didn't want to do anything at all.

When the sun had started going down, his bedroom dim enough that he began mustering the willpower to get up and turn on the lights, his phone rang. It was Kylie—he let it ring a few more times before guilt prompted him into finally answering.

"Hello?" he croaked out, his voice raspy with disuse.

"Jesus, Taylor, are you alright?" Kylie's voice came from the other end. "You sound like shit."

Taylor sighed, unsure how to answer. "Uh... I'm okay."

Kylie was silent for a moment. When she spoke again, her tone was far less teasing. "What's wrong?"

"You called me," Taylor huffed. "What do you want?"

"Mostly I wanted to make sure you were alright. You usually text me back," she replied. "You don't sound okay, though. Should I come over?"

"No," Taylor said automatically, then groaned. "Well... Maybe. I don't know."

"I'm coming over. Have you had dinner?"

"No."

"I'll pick up takeout on the way, then. Text me what you want. I'll stop at that Chinese place on the corner."

"Kylie," he started to protest, already regretting that he'd caved so quickly. "You don't have to, really."

"I'm already getting ready to leave, Taylor," she retorted. Her voice sounded more distant; she had put the phone on speaker, and he could hear rustling and movement in the background. "Don't try to lie to me. It's been long enough now that I can recognize your voice when you're spiraling, and I promised I'd get you through this. So I'm coming over."

He didn't know how to respond, sitting on the edge of his bed and blinking away tears. He didn't have the band anymore, but he'd still have Kylie. That had to count for something. She was probably the best friend he had now.

"Okay," he croaked, wiping his eyes. "Yeah. Okay. Thank you."

"I'll be there in thirty minutes," she replied, her voice softer now. "See you soon."

She hung up, and Taylor flopped back onto his bed with a groan. He didn't really feel ready to talk about what had happened with Parker, but she would surely ask what had gotten him so down again when she arrived, and he didn't want to lie to her. Maybe she would have some advice that would make him feel better, even a little.

Sighing, he forced himself to get out of bed and turned on the lights. He looked a mess, so he tidied himself up, brushing his teeth and changing into clean clothes. Dishes from days ago were still in the sink, so he set to work cleaning them off and putting them in the dishwasher. He was just turning it on when the doorbell chimed, almost immediately followed by the sound of the front door opening.

"I'm coming in!" Kylie's voice rang out from the entryway, making Taylor chuckle despite himself.

"Come on in," he called back. Kylie shuffled into the kitchen, carrying a takeout bag in one hand and a drink tray in the other; Taylor grabbed the precariously balanced tray and set it on the counter. "You didn't say you were getting boba too."

"Well, I was already there," she laughed. "I made a snap decision. I'm, like, ninety percent sure I got your order right. Taro milk tea with boba, right?"

Taylor's smile wavered with emotion. It was such a small thing, but it made him feel the first glimmer of... happiness? Hope? Something he hadn't felt since his conversation with Parker, before he'd said the words that brought it all crashing down.

Parker. The memory made his smile stutter.

"Aw, shit, did I get it wrong?" Kylie asked, her cheerful expression falling. Taylor bit back a laugh as he shook his head, rubbing his eyes with his free hand before the tears burning there could spill over.

"No, no, you got it right," he said quickly. "I just... Shit. Sorry. It isn't you."

Kylie's lips pursed with worry, as she looked at Taylor for a long moment. "You want to talk about it?"

"Maybe," Taylor sighed. "Maybe after we eat."

She nodded, and soon they were sitting in front of the TV, eating their takeout and watching an episode of some reality show Kylie was binging. He watched in silence as Kylie howled with laughter over some over-the-top argument two women were having—he still wasn't entirely sure what the show was about.

The moment Taylor finished eating, though, Kylie paused the show and turned to him with an expectant look. He couldn't stifle the laugh at that, especially because the frame she paused on was blurred with movement, save for the exaggerated, shocked expression of a man in the background.

"Okay, okay," he chuckled, before she could say anything. "It's, uh. A long story, I guess."

"Tell me," she said, leaning closer to him. First, he reached for the remote and turned the TV off. Kylie snorted with laughter when she noticed, but he was absolutely not going to have this conversation with *that* image in the corner of his eye.

"It's, um, Parker," Taylor blurted out, forcing a casual tone. But Kylie's eyes brightened immediately. She didn't say anything, and even her expression remained mostly the same, but he could practically feel the way she tensed up in anticipation at the admission. "We... talked some stuff out the other day. Or, uh... I guess it started last week."

"Start from the beginning," she prompted. "What happened?"

"Last week, I..." he started, then trailed off, his face burning with embarrassment. He'd played the moment that he'd kissed Parker over and over in his head, but it still had the sting of shame and regret remembering it now.

"I... kissed Parker." Kylie made a stifled noise, like she wanted to scream, as she clapped one hand over her mouth, eyes wide. Taylor laughed nervously, looking away. "Yeah, I know."

"Oh, Taylor, did it go badly? Is that why you've been sad?" she asked urgently, leaning forward to grab his hand, the one not in the cast.

"Er... sort of," he sighed. "I mean, I thought he wanted it—he was into it at first, and then... He kind of, uh, freaked out, but not in an 'ew, gross' way but... He was saying we shouldn't do this, that he introduced me and... me and Zach, and he would feel too guilty."

"No!" Kylie groaned, squeezing his hand harder. "Did you tell him?"

Taylor flushed, looking away. "I... Yeah. I told him. He was really... shocked, I guess. He seemed kind of upset about it, even. He said he needed to think things over, so... We didn't really talk much after that. I was... pretty upset about how he reacted. But then he still came over to work on some stuff at the venue yesterday, and..."

"Do I need to kick his ass?" Kylie interjected as he trailed off. Taylor shook his head—she looked almost disappointed.

"No, it's not like that," he sighed. "We talked it out, and I told him more about what happened, and he seemed more understanding, but then he was saying like... We shouldn't, you know, be in a relationship or whatever yet, that it's still too soon and we should... go slow. But I don't know when it won't be too soon anymore. And I explained why it isn't too soon for *me*, but I guess he doesn't feel the same way."

Kylie was silent for a long moment, brows furrowed. Finally, she hissed out, "God, he's so stupid."

Taylor laughed, even as a surge of protectiveness rose in his chest. "I guess. Maybe a little."

"You have to be more aggressive with him, Taylor," Kylie urged. "You both want this, so make it so obvious that he can't talk himself out of it. He *says* it's because he doesn't want to go too fast too soon, but I bet you anything he's just too in his head about it and psyching himself out. When has he ever dated anyone longer than a month or two? He's looked at you like you hung the fucking moon for as long as I've known him, so it's not that he doesn't have feelings for you. He's just a baby scared of things changing between you guys. But he shouldn't let that stop him, and neither should you."

Taylor was silent for a long moment. Maybe there was some truth to that. Kylie was usually a pretty sharp judge of character, and it was true that in all the years he'd known Parker, the other man hadn't ever dated anyone seriously. It had made sense each time—he traveled a lot for work, he didn't want to settle down—but as far as Taylor knew, he hadn't done more than casually date in years, if ever. Maybe he was afraid of change or commitment—not afraid of *Taylor*.

"I guess you're right," he finally relented, not meeting Kylie's gaze. "But, I mean, if he doesn't want to, I can't force him."

"I'm not saying that. I'm saying you have to call him out on his excuses. You told him it isn't too soon. If he's still saying it is, keep telling him it's not! I know it's been a while for you, or whatever, and the dynamic was really different with you and Zach, but you just gotta keep going after him, you know?"

"I... I guess so," Taylor stammered, all at once embarrassed and defensive over her judgment of the situation. Not that she was wrong. Zach had been the one who pursued Taylor, and he'd been *very* up front. Of course, he'd been entirely enamored with Zach at the time, too, so it wasn't like Zach had to chase him for long. He hadn't had to think about what it would be like to date someone for years; in contrast, Parker would have had no real frame of reference of what a long-term relationship between them might look like.

Maybe it was hopeless. Maybe they were too different now for things to work between them. Kylie seemed to pick up on the dark turn of his thoughts right away, and she added quickly,

"Don't worry too much about it right now, Taylor. Boys are stupid. He'll come around, I'm sure. Just keep making sure he knows you're still interested. Hell, maybe if you get his dick to do the thinking instead, he'll fold."

Taylor laughed aloud at that, and the mood lightened considerably. Kylie took a long drink of her boba, a sly smile on her lips. "You just gotta go with what works."

"You're right," Taylor sighed, leaning back and turning the TV back on so Kylie could finish her episode.

He mulled it over for the remainder of the evening, until Kylie went back home, and he was alone again. What was Parker so afraid of? How much clearer could Taylor be?

If nothing else, his conversation with Kylie made him certain that he had to start acting instead of just reacting. Not just with Parker, but in the rest of his life, too. He wrote a short to-do list. Parker would be out of town for interviews all the next week, so everything between them would have to wait; but there were plenty of things he could do in the meantime. Like finally getting this damn cast off his arm, once and for all.

Chapter Fourteen
Parker

Something in Parker settled after their conversation; now, at least, they knew where they stood with each other. He'd thought it had overall been a neutral interaction, but Taylor had been quiet and distant ever since, making him worry that maybe the other man was regretting how things had gone. Maybe he wasn't as into Parker as he'd hoped. Maybe Taylor was mad that Parker had wanted to take things slowly—had maybe just been looking for something immediate and casual. Although, the more he thought about it, that didn't seem like Taylor either; but the thought lingered just the same.

He was out of state all the following week for interviews in Nashville—two for Tim, and one for his own podcast. Taylor texted him a few times, but mostly it was Parker trying to initiate conversations with varying degrees of success. Still, he asked if Taylor needed his help with the venue the next week, and Taylor agreed, so things couldn't be that bad. Right?

Annoyingly, he could *hear* how distracted he sounded, listening back to the interviews to transcribe them for the articles. He hadn't realized that he'd been so distracted, but he could remember his thoughts being elsewhere during the interviews. Not that the singers he'd interviewed seemed to notice, or care.

When he got off the plane back in San Diego, he took his phone off airplane mode and got an immediate buzz—not a message from Taylor like he'd hoped, but from Kylie.

Kylie

> Heya, heard you're back in town today! We're doing a band dinner thing tonight and I figured I'd offer the invitation if you're around.

He blinked down at his phone for a long moment, confused—then shuffled out of the way self-consciously, realizing he'd been standing right in the center of the walkway for the baggage claim. He and Kylie were friends, sure, but it surprised him that the invitation came from her and not Taylor.

But he didn't have plans, and it would beat having to cook dinner himself after a day of traveling.

Parker

> Sure, thanks for the invite. Let me know when and where.

By the time he'd gotten his luggage and made his way back to his car, Kylie had texted him back.

Kylie

> Great! Don't tell Taylor. We're surprising him.

Parker laughed—he'd been just about to text Taylor that he was back and looking forward to seeing him tonight, so her text had come just in time. Instead, he replied that he wouldn't tell, then sent Taylor a shorter text to let him know he was back in town.

Taylor called him while he was driving home.

"Hey!" Parker exclaimed. "Good to hear from you."

"Glad you got home safe," Taylor's voice came from his car speakers. "I, uh, I wanted to ask you something."

Parker's heart skipped a beat. "Sure, what's up?"

"I... I made an appointment to get this cast off, finally," he replied. "It's for next week, and, uh, I was wondering if you'd maybe take me there."

"Yeah!" Parker exclaimed far too quickly—he wasn't even sure what his schedule was going to be like next week. But Taylor was important; he'd move his schedule around if he had to. "Yeah, for sure. I'll take you. Just tell me when, and I'll be there."

Taylor let out a faint laugh, crackly over the speaker. "Thanks. I really appreciate it."

"Of course," Parker replied. "Anything you need, seriously."

Taylor was quiet for a long moment before answering. "I—I know. Yeah. Anyway, uh, how was your trip?"

Relief squeezed in his chest. At least he didn't seem to be pulling away anymore.

"It was good," Parker replied. "Had some interesting interviews. Nashville's always fun."

"Anyone I know?" Taylor asked. It was the most normal conversation that they'd had in weeks.

"Uh, probably not," he replied with a laugh. "Actually, one of my interviews was for my podcast, this up and coming trans country singer. He's gotten super popular in the past six months or so. Might be good to keep him in mind when you start booking for the Caesura Room. William Kaye. I was listening to his stuff on the plane ride over, it was really good."

"Yeah, send me the link. I'll give it a listen," Taylor replied.

They were both silent for a moment, then Taylor continued, "I, uh, I'll let you go. I can tell you're driving."

Parker chuckled. "Okay. See you soon."

/ /

Dinner was at a small, new gastropub downtown that Parker had never been to before. He gave Kylie's name to the hostess, and she led him out to a small balcony with only a few tables, one of which was occupied by Kylie, Dean, and Angie. There were only four chairs at the table, so he stepped toward the empty one.

"Hey," he greeted them, hoping Taylor would arrive soon. With any luck, Dean wouldn't be as weird to him as he had been last time.

"Hey, Parker!" Kylie chirped as he sat down next to her. "Glad you could make it."

"Thanks for the invite," he replied, smiling nervously. All three of them were looking at him; Kylie's expression seemed somehow overly cheerful. Already, something didn't seem right. "What's, uh, what's the occasion?"

"No occasion, really," Kylie replied quickly. But Parker caught the way Dean and Angie glanced at her as she spoke, like following a cue, which only made him more unsettled. "I've heard this place was good and figured this was as good an excuse as any to check it out, you know?"

"Sure," he said, shrugging. A waiter came by to get their orders before he could say anything else; he thought they might wait for Taylor, but the others ordered drinks, so he ordered a beer, too.

They sat there in silence for a beat after the waiter left, then Parker offered, "What have you guys been up to since last time?"

Dean only shrugged; he was looking down at the table now, not quite ignoring Parker, but not looking at him now either. Angie replied,

"Not much, to be honest. We've been putting out feelers with some people we know who are making music to see about starting new projects, but honestly, it's kind of been nice to be taking a break from it all. I just finished PT for my ankle, too, so that's been a relief."

Kylie was biting her lip as Angie spoke; before Parker could reply to her, though, Kylie interrupted,

"What about you, Parker?"

Parker blinked owlishly; it was an innocuous enough question, but something in her tone made it seem... more than just that.

Did she know about him and Taylor? Cold sweat beaded on the back of his neck; if she did know, what was she trying to get at, asking him such an open-ended question? What did she want him to say?

"Uh, the usual," he replied, trying to sound casual. "I just got back from doing some interviews in Nashville. Oh, did I tell you about the interview I had with Jason Daugherty? He's putting out a new album with Synesthesia—"

"Shit, really?" Dean asked with a surprised laugh, the first words he'd spoken to Parker, which only threw him off more. "How did that go?"

"Surprisingly well," he replied with a nervous chuckle. "He's sober for now, and it seems like it might stick this time, so..."

"That's cool," Kylie said, still looking at him intently, obviously not finding what she wanted to hear. She *had* to be fishing for something about him and Taylor, but what? And why now?

"So, uh... When's Taylor getting here?" he asked uncertainly.

Kylie finally glanced away, looking over at the siblings. The three of them shared a long look, then finally Kylie turned back to Parker.

"Actually, Taylor's not coming," she said with a grim expression.

Parker blinked, processing. "He's not? I thought you said—"

"We're staging an intervention, Parker!" Kylie interrupted, stomping one foot on the ground under the table. "You're this close to fucking everything up with Taylor! And I'm not going to sit and watch you blow it all up."

Heat flooded Parker's face in confused embarrassment, his mouth working silently. What was she even saying? How was he supposed to respond to that? "I—What? What are you talking about?"

"Kylie told us about you and Taylor," Angie offered, holding a hand out to Kylie, who was huffing in frustration. "And we wanted to help, uh, make Taylor's situation more clear."

"Situation? What?" he stammered, still confused. What the hell was going on?

"Seriously?" Kylie scowled. "Don't play dumb. I talked to Taylor, and I know what happened with you guys. Are you dating or not?"

His heart threatened to explode out of his chest. His eyes darted between all three of them—Kylie frowning, Angie carefully neutral, Dean annoyed.

"N-No?" he offered uncertainly. This, however, was clearly not the answer Kylie wanted to hear: she huffed and folded her arms across her chest in response.

"Why *not*?" she pressed. "Seriously? Why are you stringing him along like this?"

"I'm—I'm not!" he protested, shaking his head. "It's, you know, it's complicated."

"I think maybe it's not as complicated as you're making it out to be, Parker," Angie said, smiling nervously at him. "Taylor really likes you, and it seems like you like him, so there's not really anything stopping you guys from being together, if that's what you both want."

Parker pressed his hands to his face, cheeks burning. Was this really why they'd invited him to dinner? To interrogate him about Taylor? The jumble of shame and irritation and betrayal was too overwhelming for him to string together a sentence, so he only rubbed his face for a moment, unable to respond. Kylie added,

"You really hurt his feelings, you know."

"What?" he burst out, glaring at her. "What did I do?"

"Parker!" she bit back. "You're almost thirty, dude. Do you really think you can tell someone who's been practically throwing themselves at you that you want to back off and slow down, and *not* make them feel like you're letting them down easy?"

"It isn't like that," he stammered. "I just... I mean, all the stuff I said before that—and what did he even tell you, anyway?"

"That he made it clear he wants to be with you," Kylie answered. "And he told you everything about him and Zach. And that still wasn't good enough for you!"

"That isn't—It isn't like that," he repeated. His heart was pounding in his chest. "I just said I didn't want to, you know, jump into anything without being sure. It's only been, what, four months? I just—I don't want Taylor to do anything he'll regret later."

"They would have been broken up for over a year now, Parker," Angie said. "It's not like a rebound thing for him at this point."

"Exactly! That shouldn't be an excuse," Kylie agreed. "So what's really the problem, Parker?"

Parker was silent for a long moment, looking at Kylie with consternation. Taylor would never have put them up to this weird intervention, so why were they going after him like this?

"This is—This is stupid," he finally stammered. His protests clearly didn't convince Kylie, though, who continued to glare at him. "Why do you even care? It's between me and Taylor."

"Yeah, well, Taylor is our friend," Kylie snapped. "And I'm not going to let you hurt him even worse! This has already been tough enough on him without you messing this up."

"I'm not messing anything up!"

"We just want to see Taylor happy," Angie interjected, her voice still low and calm compared to Kylie. "And if it takes us nudging you in the right direction, well..."

"I don't need to be *nudged*," Parker groaned. He would have protested further, but the waiter arrived with their drinks then, so the table fell awkwardly quiet as he passed them out.

"Ready to order?" the waiter asked cheerfully, seemingly oblivious to the tension between the four of them. A beat of silence passed, then Angie replied with a smile,

"I think we're going to need a few more minutes."

Parker took a long sip of his drink to avoid having to say any more, scowling down at his glass.

"Look, dude," Dean said, startling Parker. "We're only doing this because we know you make Taylor happy. If you don't want to be with him, stop stringing him along. If you do, quit playing fucking hard to get with him, before he decides he's better off alone."

Parker stared, at a loss for words. Would that really happen? He thought he'd made it clear that he just wanted to *wait* before acting on anything, but was Taylor that ready to move on?

"You don't need to wait for him to be ready, Parker," Kylie said, her voice gentler now. "He's *ready*. Are you?"

"I..." he started, only to trail off. Was he? The prospect of being in a relationship with Taylor filled his chest with anticipation and excitement—and, when he took a moment to sort through the feelings, fear. What would happen if they got together, then things didn't go well? "I don't... I don't know."

"What are you unsure about?" Kylie asked. "He's not going to say no to you, Parker."

"I know that," Parker replied, shaking his head. To put the feelings jumbling around in his chest into words was an impossible task. "I just... Me and Zach are nothing alike, you know? He was a fucking *rock star*. And I'm just... A regular guy. I write about music because I was never... never good enough to make it."

Angie's lips pursed in a sympathetic expression. Dean's gaze lingered on the menu propped in front of him, but Kylie's expression remained carefully neutral. Shame burned his face at the admission—it felt silly to have said it aloud—but maybe that was the crux of the issue, or as close to it as Parker could verbalize.

"He wasn't a rock star when they got together," Kylie finally said, her voice firm. "He was a college kid with the batshit belief that he was *going* to be a rock star someday. It ended up being true for him, sure; but it doesn't change the fact that he was just a regular guy first, too. He had a wild dream he was willing to drop *everything* for. And Taylor wanted to go along for the ride, however it turned out. They didn't know he would be a rock star then. He wasn't for most of their relationship."

"I fucking introduced them," Parker interrupted, pain dripping from his voice. "How fucked up is that? I introduced them. I got them together. Then as soon as he's gone, I try to swoop in and—and—"

He couldn't even finish the thought. It felt so sleazy, so *wrong*, that all his other misgivings paled in comparison. Zach had been his friend, and now he was gone. Getting together with his husband was a betrayal to both of them, even knowing everything Taylor had told him now.

The others were silent for a beat—then Dean snorted, sending a painful shock of indignant anger through Parker's chest. He glared over at Dean, who met him with a cold look.

"Seriously, dude? You're only doing this because of some made-up version of Zach you have in your head," Dean said, the irritation obvious in his voice. "I know you think they were great together and whatever, but they hadn't been involved for *months* before Zach died. The real Zach would have been stoked Taylor was seeing someone, if he were alive right now, especially if it were you. You were his friend, both of their friends. He would have known you'd treat Taylor well, and now you have the chance, and you're letting it blow up in your face? Get your shit together, man."

It was as if he'd been struck by lightning. Parker wanted to be angry—wanted to spit back that Dean had no idea what he was talking about—that he was way overstepping their barely amicable relationship.

But maybe he was right. Dean and Zach had been close friends—closer than Zach and Parker, at least. And it was his friend who had been seeing Zach after Zach and Taylor split up. Dean didn't even really have a personal stake in anything Taylor did now, so maybe his take was the most unbiased.

Maybe the image Parker had in his head was further from reality than he thought. Maybe Zach and Taylor hadn't been as perfect for each other as they'd seemed from the outside. Maybe Taylor really wanted him, the same way he'd wanted Taylor all this time. Maybe if he didn't act soon, he really would lose Taylor altogether—their friendship with it. If he was going to lose Taylor as a friend if he *didn't* act on their feelings, wouldn't it be better to just take the risk?

Wouldn't it?

Angie hissed something under her breath at Dean that he didn't quite catch. Dean muttered something back to her, then Angie turned to Parker.

"Sorry, Parker," she said. "He shouldn't have said it that way. But, well..."

"He's right," Kylie said bluntly. "It's tough love, Parker. We're doing this because we *want* you to get it together. We want to see Taylor happy. And you make him happy, at least for now, so..."

"I get it," Parker interrupted, his voice coming out as a hoarse croak. "Really, guys, I... I get it. You're right. I didn't... I don't think I really understood until now."

"Told you," Dean muttered. Angie reached over and smacked his bare arm hard, making him yowl and shrink away. "Dammit! That hurt."

"Good," Angie hissed again between her teeth, then looked at Parker again. "We just wanted to help, Parker. At least Kylie and I did. Taylor would never be this, uh... *forward* about his feelings, I think. So we had to do it for him."

Parker nodded, watching the three of them. Dean had looked away, rubbing his arm with a scowl; but he didn't look as angry as he had before his outburst. Kylie was staring at him silently, but a tiny smile ghosted at the corners of her deep red-stained lips. She recognized the change in Parker already, and whatever she had been hoping for from this conversation, it seemed like she had gotten it.

"You guys are good friends," Parker blurted out, making Kylie grin and Angie laugh. "To Taylor, I mean. Really. I don't think I have anyone who would have done this for me. I'm... I'm glad he has so many people around who love him. I know he and Zach weren't together, but this has still been hard on him, so..."

"Trust us, we know," Kylie sighed, before taking a sip of her drink.

"It's definitely thrown a wrench in everything, that's for sure," Dean muttered, glaring at the ground sullenly.

"We all miss Zach," Angie said softly. "I think we always will. And it's complicated for Taylor. Don't hold that against him."

"I don't. I wouldn't," Parker said quickly, shaking his head. "I miss Zach too. Even knowing all this now... Fuck, it almost feels like it would be simpler if he were still here, huh?"

"Yeah. I think so, too," Kylie agreed, her smile faltering.

They sat in pensive silence for a moment. As if recognizing the lull, their waiter appeared once more, and this time they put in a food order after all. When he was gone, Kylie turned to Parker again, the same mischievous smile on her face.

"So when are you going to ask Taylor on a real date this time?" she prompted, and Parker flushed, laughing nervously.

"I, uh," he stammered, still not quite sure. "Well, I'm taking him to a doctor's appointment next week to finally get his cast off, so... Maybe after that."

"I can't believe he still has that on! Poor guy," Angie exclaimed, shaking her head. "I hated that stupid boot I had to wear. He's going to be so relieved once it's finally off."

Parker nodded, smiling weakly. "I think so, too. It's been a long time coming."

"I'd better hear good news from Taylor after his appointment, then," Kylie said matter-of-factly, and Parker snorted with laughter. A terrible pressure in his chest had been lifted and drained away, leaving him light and airy now. It still made him nervous to think of really *being* with Taylor, but knowing how much everyone was rooting for him, for *them*, helped him feel more confident than he had before.

"You will. I promise," he said softly, and she smiled approvingly.

"Great," she said, and took another sip of her drink before adding, "Thanks for being such a good sport. Dinner's on me, bud."

Chapter Fifteen
Taylor

THEN

"Hey, uh, can we talk?"

Taylor blinked, turning to face Zach, who was standing awkwardly in the open doorway of the music room. The other man had an obviously conflicted expression on his face, and he was tugging on a strand of his hair, a telltale sign he was nervous. Uncertainly, Taylor pulled his hands away from the keyboard and swiveled in his chair to face the other man fully.

"Sure," he said, gesturing for Zach to come in. He stepped carefully into the room; it was somehow messier now with only Taylor's things in it, compared to when it housed equipment belonging to both of them. Taylor had pulled out several of the keyboards that he'd previously had in storage, testing them to make sure they all still worked—half of them were still set up around the room, making the whole space a maze.

"What's up?" Taylor prompted, after Zach stood there in the middle of the room for a long moment, his blue eyes lingering on the spot on the wall where one of his guitars had once been mounted.

"I wanted you to be the first to know," Zach finally said, still not quite looking at him. "I mean, I know we agreed it was fine and all, but... Still. I didn't want you to hear it from anyone else. But I'm, uh... I've been seeing someone. It hasn't been super, like, serious, but we just decided to be exclusive, so... It might get more serious. And I wanted to make sure you knew."

He finally looked at Taylor, meeting his eyes with apprehension. Taylor stared at him blankly for a long moment.

He was surprised, sure, but... It didn't hurt. It didn't make him sad, or upset, or jealous. Well, maybe a touch jealous—not for Zach, but for the fact that he'd been the first between them to find someone else. Mostly, he was curious about who this other person was, and... that was it.

The smile spreading across his face startled him into action, and he replied quickly, "Thanks for telling me. I'm happy for you."

Zach returned the smile hesitantly. "Yeah?"

"Yeah," Taylor replied, nodding. "And I appreciate the heads up, seriously. It's better to hear it from you, for sure."

Zach's grin widened. "I figured. And I didn't really think you'd be, you know, upset or anything, but I guess I was still... Nervous. To tell you. Is that weird?"

Taylor laughed, shaking his head. "No, that makes sense. But we're good. No worries."

Taylor was certain then that they weren't in love anymore. He hadn't really thought so for a while, but this only confirmed it. He was happy that his friend found someone who made him happy, with no desire to be that object of affection anymore. Once, he might have burned alive with jealousy at the thought of Zach with someone else, but now it was just... fine. Ambivalent.

It was a relief, in a strange way. A confirmation that they had made the right decision.

"So who is it? Anyone I know?" Taylor asked, making Zach chuckle and glance away shyly.

"Yeah, uh, do you remember Dean's friend Rogelio?" he asked. "I'd been hanging out at Dean and Angie's place more, and me and Rogelio kind of reconnected during a get-together they had, and... It just sort of snowballed from there."

"Yeah, I remember him," Taylor said, grinning. He'd only met Rogelio maybe two or three times, but he could vaguely recall the tall man with a narrow, angular face, short dark hair kept in a clean fade, and silver piercings in both ears and nostrils. He could certainly imagine the two of them together, a pair of lanky, handsome punk princes. The vision made him chuckle.

"You don't have to answer, but have you been, you know, seeing anyone?" Zach asked, his tone careful now. Taylor hesitated, glancing away with some embarrassment.

"No, I haven't," he answered honestly, shaking his head. Dating was far too daunting—he was about to enter a new phase in his life, and trying to meet someone now was poor timing at best. Once he was more settled into himself, and what it meant to no longer be a touring musician, maybe then he'd start looking, but... "To be honest, man, dating apps scare the shit out of me. Everything about dating and meeting people is just... so different from when we were in college, you know?"

Zach laughed, nodding. "That's for fucking sure." The tattoo under his eye crinkled with his smile. "Well, uh, I have some unsolicited advice for you in that regard."

Taylor snorted. "Seriously, dude?"

"You want to hear it or not?"

"Fine, fine," he laughed, gesturing for Zach to continue. The other man bit his lip, still half-smiling, as if considering what it was he actually wanted to say.

"I'm, like, almost a hundred percent positive Parker has always had a crush on you," he finally said. Taylor gave a start—whatever he'd been expecting Zach to say, *that* certainly was not it. "So, you know, if you want to avoid all the dating app shit..."

"Parker? Really?" Taylor laughed, feeling his face flaming with heat. Parker was a sweetheart, sure, and a good-looking one at that, but... Really? He wondered if Zach somehow knew about his on and off attraction to Parker. He couldn't imagine Parker seeing him that way.

"Damn, poor guy's not even here to defend himself," Zach said, lifting his hands in an appeasing gesture, making Taylor laugh—probably too loud, too nervously.

"No, it's not that, I just—I never would have thought," he said quickly. "It's... It's funny you say that, honestly, because I've always thought he's cute. I had a little bit of a crush on him when we first met, but he never made a move, and then he introduced me to you, so... I figured he wasn't interested, you know?"

Zach laughed, shaking his head. "Oh, god, don't tell me I've been cockblocking this guy for a decade."

"No, no!" Taylor protested. They were both laughing, but some small part of him was suddenly rethinking every interaction that he and Parker had ever shared. Parker was handsome and had always been kind to him, and he enjoyed reading Parker's articles and his blog—he'd even listened to most of his podcast episodes—but had never really considered Parker might think the same about him.

Well, once the summer tour was over and things were officially ended with Zach, maybe he would revisit the prospect of Parker. Maybe there was something there after all.

"Anyway, that's all I wanted to say," Zach finally said. "Hope that isn't too weird."

Taylor shook his head. "Not at all. Thanks for telling me."

Zach looked at him a moment longer, worrying his lower lip between his teeth—the movement made the small divots where his snakebites used to be more visible. After a beat, Zach added,

"Taylor, I... I just want you to know I'm really glad things worked out the way they did. I still care about you, and I hope we can still be friends after all this. I understand that some space from each other will probably be good, but... I don't know. I don't know what I'm trying to say."

Taylor's gaze softened. He had a similar strange fondness toward Zach too—not quite affection, but stronger than friendship. It was weird to think of Zach as his ex when they still had such positive feelings for each other, but he was also entirely sure that whatever they had between them now was not romantic in the least. Still, Zach's words made his heart constrict with emotion.

"I know," Taylor replied, nodding. "I understand. Me, too."

11

Now

There were still things Taylor needed to do to make sure everything was set up for the venue, but he found himself putting them off all week. His mind was always elsewhere—either wondering about Parker, or worrying about finally getting his cast off. Such a childish concern, but he couldn't shake it.

After so long, he was almost afraid of seeing his arm underneath the cast. How badly would his muscles have atrophied? Would he need physical therapy? Would he be able to play the piano again? Even if he didn't want to be making music anymore, playing piano had been a constant in his life since childhood, one he couldn't imagine ever giving up fully.

Parker was texting him more often since he'd gotten back in town from his week in Tennessee, as if he somehow knew how despondent Taylor had felt about their last conversation. Anxiety tightened in his throat when he thought about how everything might still play out, but he also couldn't deny how he liked the attention—the way Parker would text him good morning and good night, and would often call during the day so they could chat. Even though Parker had said he wanted to wait, it still felt like they were right on the precipice of *something*, and the anticipation was as pleasant as it was exhilarating.

But then he would think about the cast and his arm again, and his positive feelings would fizzle away into worry. Still, it was nice while it lasted.

The day of his appointment arrived eventually; he barely slept the night before, his stomach twisting with nerves the whole time. It made no sense to be so anxious, but when had his heart ever listened to sense?

Luckily, his appointment was in the morning, so he didn't have to spend half the day waiting around nervously. Parker texted him when he arrived at the house; he had a to-go cup of coffee held out to him when Taylor climbed into his car.

"For you," Parker said with a nervous smile, making Taylor grin back.

"I think my heart might explode if I drink this," he said, but accepted it anyway and took a careful sip—it was a white chocolate mocha with nonfat milk and no whipped cream, his usual order. Taylor's heart fluttered with pleasure this time, realizing Parker remembered it now. "Thank you."

"Don't be nervous," Parker said, still smiling. "I had a cast off when I was a kid, and the blade doesn't even reach your skin. Once they cut through the hard part, they use scissors for the bandage parts."

Taylor smiled weakly. That wasn't really what he was nervous about, but he didn't know how to put his worries into words—he wasn't even entirely sure what exactly had him so anxious.

"Yeah," he agreed faintly, looking out the window. "You're right."

They drove in silence for a while, save for the music playing. Parker seemed nervous too, but Taylor wasn't sure how much of that might have been him projecting.

"You know, I don't have any plans after this," Parker finally said during a lull in the music. "I was thinking it would be nice to maybe get lunch or something afterward... If you want to hang out."

Taylor smiled. Having something to look forward to after the appointment would help. "Yeah, that sounds good. Do you have any places in mind?"

Parker shrugged. "There are some decent spots near the doctor's office, or we can head back closer to your place if you'd prefer."

"Whatever's fine," Taylor said, shaking his head. He had no appetite at all, at least not now. Hopefully he'd feel differently once this was over.

They arrived at the doctor's office soon after that. For a long moment after they'd parked, Taylor sat motionless, looking out the window toward the building, unable to shake the dread that had welled up in the back of his throat.

"You alright?" Parker asked softly. The car was off, and the music had gone silent, but he was looking at Taylor with his brows furrowed and his hand hovering over the handle of the car door.

"Uh, yeah," Taylor stammered, quickly unbuckling himself and hurrying out of the car. "Sorry. Kind of zoned out there."

Parker frowned, worry tinging his previously light-hearted expression. "You're sure?"

Taylor hesitated, unsure how to say what he was thinking. "I'm just nervous, I guess. It's silly. But it feels... weird. Is it stupid that I'm, like... scared to get it off, almost? Not because it'll hurt, or whatever, but... I don't know. It feels like this huge change."

Parker's gaze softened with sympathy, making Taylor's heart beat faster. "It's not stupid. I get it. It *is* a change, for sure."

Taylor smiled weakly. "Yeah."

Parker stood hesitantly beside him for a moment, then reached over to put a hand on his back in a comforting, if uncertain, gesture. Taylor leaned into the contact, the touch soothing.

"You got this," Parker said softly. "I bet you're going to be so relieved when it's off."

Taylor nodded, but his brows remained furrowed; the thought brought him no relief now. "Yeah, you're right."

They walked together into the doctor's office, and Taylor waited in line for the receptionist as Parker sat down in the waiting room. Taylor joined him once he'd checked in, heart still pounding. Parker rubbed his back again, and Taylor leaned closer to him—now that Parker had touched him, he couldn't imagine that anything else could possibly help him feel better.

"So what are you thinking for lunch?" Taylor forced out, and Parker smirked in response.

"Wherever you want," he replied. "But if you're asking me to pick... There's a good place not too far from here I've been to a couple of times. Sunny Side Up, have you ever been there?"

Taylor shook his head, trying to focus on Parker's words. "No, but that sounds like a brunch place."

"Yeah, they have this great peanut butter and jelly French toast," Parker said. "But their regular lunch stuff is good too. Or, oh, there's that brewery closer to your place. They have really good lunch. Are you feeling more sweet or savory?"

"Ask me again when I have this off," Taylor chuckled weakly, gesturing with his right hand. The last thing he could think about right now was food.

"Taylor?" a nurse called from the open door, startling Taylor to his feet.

"Want me to come with you?" Parker asked softly, and Taylor nodded rapidly before he'd fully processed the question. Still, Parker stood without complaint and followed as the nurse led them to the back.

"Oh, you were supposed to get this off ages ago!" she tutted as they walked through the halls, looking down at a clipboard that she held in one hand. Taylor's chest constricted. "I bet you're thrilled to finally be getting it removed, huh?"

"Uh, yeah," he stammered. Parker's hand met the small of his back, warm and strong, and he added in a more normal tone, "I just missed my appointment to get it off and procrastinated making a new one, I guess. I know that was probably bad, but..."

The nurse smiled over her shoulder at him. "In most cases, it shouldn't make a difference. If your doctor recommended PT when you had the cast put on, that should take care of any stiffness, so there wouldn't be a significant difference between then and now. Alright, have a seat right here, and your friend can take that chair."

She gestured for Taylor to sit on an examination chair, then pointed at a smaller chair in the corner for Parker. Parker scooted the chair closer to Taylor, so they were sitting next to each other. The nurse's eyes lingered on them for a beat, but otherwise she made no comment as she set up the saw.

"Now, I know it sounds scary, but the blade can't hurt you. It's actually just vibrations that break the cast apart, so it can't cut the skin at all," she explained. "You'll probably feel a bit of pressure, but at most it might tickle you. It's loud, though, so feel free to put in headphones or earplugs if that would bother you. And let me know if you need a little break."

Taylor gulped, nodding. "Okay."

She pulled up a chair on the other side of him, holding the saw. "Ready?" she asked cheerfully.

He glanced at Parker, who gave him an encouraging smile. It was so stupid—he felt like a child, having to be assuaged that he wouldn't be harmed. But it wasn't that he was worried about being hurt. The thought of finally being without the cast filled him with... He couldn't even name the feeling, only that his stomach churned with nausea. Like once the cast was off, his life would be irrevocably changed in a way that he would never get back.

"Ready," he replied faintly, holding out his arm. The saw clicked on, its loud whirr filling the room. Parker's hand squeezed his—he hadn't even noticed Parker reaching for it. His breathing sped up as the nurse gingerly grasped his arm with the other hand, tilting it slightly to get a better angle, before pressing the saw onto it. She started near his elbow, and he could feel the vibrations of it buzzing up through his shoulder. It did mostly tickle, with some pressure as the saw bit through the hard outer shell and pressed into the soft bandages below.

A choked laugh escaped him at the strange feeling, but his eyes were stinging with tears. This part of his life was really over—the last remnant of his life before Zach died would be gone.

It's over, he thought, watching her slowly press the saw further down his arm, inch by careful inch. When they'd put the cast on him, he hadn't known yet that Zach was dead. They didn't tell him until after he was fully treated.

It was all he'd had left of his time with Zach, and he could finally name the emotion flooding his chest as grief, mourning the strange finality of it. He missed Zach, not as his husband, but as his friend. He thought he'd made his peace with it, but maybe some part of him had still been holding on to the memory, hiding away in his subconscious, tied to the image of himself in a cast on that early morning after the crash.

What must Parker think of him? Did he think Taylor was a baby, on the verge of tears from something seemingly so simple and painless? Had he somehow picked up on its connection to Zach, and was now wondering if everything Taylor had told him was a lie? He couldn't bring himself to look at the other man, his mind racing with all the awful possibilities, unable to bear the prospect of Parker looking at him now with derision.

"Alright, done with the saw," the nurse said once all the plaster was cracked open in a neat line. Her eyes flickered up to his face, and her brow contorted with worry. "Oh, hon, what's the matter?"

"It's—it's nothing," he replied, shaking his head. His voice quavered, and he cleared his throat before adding, "I'm okay. Go ahead."

She hesitated for a moment, then set down the saw. Beside him, Parker leaned closer, now holding Taylor's hand in both of his. Taylor almost flinched away, but his touch was gentle enough to be soothing, yet still firm enough to show his support.

"Almost done," he said softly, his voice only nurturing, only caring. "You're okay."

He was still the same sweet, thoughtful Parker as always—it wasn't fair of Taylor to assume he'd be otherwise. Taylor watched the nurse set aside the saw and pull out what looked like a pair of pliers, but with a broader, blunt tip.

"This will spread the cast apart, to make it easier to cut the bandages and pull everything off," she explained, still using the same light tone. "Again, nothing should hurt, but you might feel a little pressure as the cast opens up. Sure you don't need a break?"

"No, I'm alright," he said. His heart was beating painfully fast in his chest, and his eyes still stung with unshed tears; but now that the process had started, he just wanted it over with—like ripping off a bandaid. She set to work, prying the now-split edges of the cast further apart. It squeezed his arm as the gap widened, and despite himself, he tried wiggling his wrist just a bit, the sensation strange and new with how long it had been held immobile in the cast.

"Alright. Last is the scissors," she continued, holding up a pair of scissors with the blade at an angle so they could press against his skin safely. "With the angle, none of the sharp parts should touch you, but I'll go slow and you tell me if you feel a pinch or anything. Ready?"

He nodded, and she slipped the blade beneath the layer of soft cotton bandages. The scissors sliced through it easily. In just a few clips of the blade, the cotton was fully split, and his arm was visible underneath. The nurse gently pulled the mess of bandage and plaster away, and he could see his bare arm for the first time in months.

It was visibly skinnier than his other forearm now, and the skin between his wrist and his elbow was dry and pink. He tentatively flexed his wrist, and his long-dormant muscles ached with disuse, making his heart sink. Had he waited too long? Would he ever be able to play the piano again?

The nurse must have been able to read the despair in his expression as she cleaned up the debris of the cast, placing it all in a disposal bin. "I see a bit of loss of muscle tone, but that's not unusual for how long you had it in the cast. I'll have the doctor come in to see if you need physical therapy, and she can send a referral today if she decides you need it. That dry skin is totally normal, too, and should clear up a lot after a few washes. Just make sure to use a gentle lotion.

You'll probably have some muscle pain for the first day or two as your arm wakes up, but any kind of regular painkiller should keep it manageable. Any pain will go away on its own in time, so don't worry too much, hon."

"Do you think..." he croaked out, tears threatening to spill from his eyelids now. "Do you think I'll play piano again?"

She sighed, sympathy flaring in her eyes. "Well, the doctor will probably be able to give you a better assessment than me, but I think you probably will. You just have to give it time, just like how you had to give it time to heal. The muscle has to build back up, but your muscle memory is still all there."

He nodded, sniffling. Finally, he tore his eyes away from the sad sight of his forearm and looked at Parker. The other man smiled at him tentatively, squeezing his hand again.

"You did it!" he said in a soft, cheering tone. Taylor laughed, but it morphed into a cry—his arm ached as he instinctively raised it to cover his mouth. "Aw, Taylor... It's okay."

He nodded, but couldn't quite stop the tears now that they'd broken the barrier. He leaned closer to Parker, who released his grip on Taylor's free hand to instead wrap his arms around Taylor's frame, hugging him tightly as he tried to stifle his cries in Parker's shoulder. The other man was murmuring something soft and comforting in his ear, but he couldn't make it out over the rush of emotion flooding through him.

His life had changed completely. The rushing undercurrent of *it's over, it's over* repeated in his mind to the rhythm of his pounding heart, the only thing he could really make sense of in the painful jumble of emotions. There was no going back now.

"You're gonna play again, Taylor," Parker was saying gently when he could focus again. He was rubbing Taylor's back in soothing circles with one hand, the other wrapped firmly around his waist. "You're gonna be able to play in time for the last show, then you'll be able to play whenever you want, for whatever you want to do afterward. Everything's going to be okay. You'll be okay."

Taylor squeezed him back, hugging him desperately. How could he have ever thought Parker would see him with anything other than the same kindness and support he'd always had? They held each other for a long moment, until Taylor thought he might be able to speak without bursting into tears again.

"S-Sorry," he finally choked out, leaning back and releasing Parker so he could wipe his eyes. The other man had a dark spot on his shirt where Taylor's tears had dampened the fabric, but he only had eyes for Taylor, watching him attentively. "I'm, uh, I'm okay. It was... I mean, I don't really know how to—how to put it into words, you know?"

Parker's eyes took on a knowing, sympathetic expression. "Yeah. I understand."

The nurse must have stepped out while Taylor was crying, because it was only the two of them in the room now.

"She said she'll be back in a minute," Parker said, noticing him looking around. He was still rubbing Taylor's back, and Taylor leaned closer to him again, reaching for his other hand. "And the doctor will come by to talk to you about physical therapy. So don't worry about it too much for now, okay?"

"It's not that," Taylor replied, shaking his head. "Well... Maybe partly. But... I don't know. We can talk about it later."

"Do you still want to get lunch?" Parker asked softly.

"Maybe we can order delivery," Taylor replied with a faint laugh. "Can we go to your place? I don't... I don't want to be in the house yet, I think."

Parker was quiet for a minute, as if the request had taken him by surprise, though it didn't show on his face.

"Yeah," he finally replied, nodding. "Yeah, of course. Whatever you want. Taylor, I..."

He trailed off, color rising in his face as he glanced up at Taylor. He still had one arm wrapped around Taylor's waist, their fingers intertwined; his grip on Taylor's hand tightened as their eyes met.

Taylor wanted to kiss him again, and the way Parker was looking at him made him think the other man wanted it too, but he was certain his face was smeared with tears and snot, so he held back. Instead, he forced a watery smile.

"Thanks for coming with me," he said softly, and Parker smiled in return.

Chapter Sixteen
Parker

Parker watched quietly as the doctor examined Taylor's arm, then explained the process of getting a referral for physical therapy. She seemed confident that any residual stiffness would go away easily, and he'd be playing piano again soon, which seemed to comfort Taylor a bit. But he still had a worried expression as they walked out of the clinic and back to Parker's car.

Taylor remained quiet and pensive during the drive back, this time heading for Parker's apartment. Parker's arms still tingled with the warmth of holding Taylor; they would talk about that, too, when they got to his place, or at least he hoped they would.

Anticipation buzzed in his chest at the thought. He kept glancing over at Taylor, curled in on himself in the passenger seat, wondering what the other man was thinking—if the ghost of their embrace still clung to his body, too.

Halfway there, Taylor finally seemed to shake himself out of whatever stupor he was in and pulled up his phone, still favoring his left hand.

"I'll, uh, I'll put in an order to your apartment now," he said quickly, sounding self-conscious. "What should we get?"

"Whatever you want," Parker replied quickly, shaking his head. "I'm not picky. Plus, you deserve to get whatever you want. Just let me know what you decide, and I'll find something on the menu I'll eat."

Taylor let out a half-hearted huff of a laugh. "Okay. I know it's basically lunchtime, but I keep thinking about all the brunch stuff we talked about. Is it weird I really want a chocolate chip waffle like my mom used to make?"

Parker laughed. "Not weird at all. I'm not sure of any places that do a chocolate chip waffle, though."

He paused, thinking as Taylor scrolled through his phone. "Actually, I have a waffle maker at home... No promises on chocolate chips, though. Or waffle mix, to be honest."

This time, Taylor really did laugh. He looked over at Parker with a watery smile, some of the tension in his body relaxing. "No way. I'm not letting you cook for me after taking me to this appointment. I'm getting you lunch, my treat."

Parker's heart skipped a beat at Taylor's laugh, seeing his mood improving. "Alright, alright. Just something to keep in mind if you can't find your chocolate chip waffles."

By the time they arrived back at Parker's apartment, Taylor had put in an order with a brunch cafe that did, in fact, have a chocolate chip waffle, plus some eggs, bacon, and a sandwich with fries for Parker. The food was set to arrive in half an hour, leaving them with some time to kill; not that he didn't enjoy hanging out with Taylor, but the anticipation of it was making Parker nervous now. They had so much to talk about, so much he wanted to say, especially after everything that had happened with Kylie and the rest of the band—but he didn't think now would be a good time to bring it all up. But if not now, when?

Maybe Taylor would start the conversation. Maybe he should let Taylor take the lead... But that was what had gotten him into such hot water with Kylie in the first place. Maybe he would just wait until after they had their food and see how Taylor was feeling then. Surely he'd be feeling better after they'd eaten, right?

The thoughts were swirling in his head as they walked in silence from the parking lot up the stairs to his apartment, but luckily Taylor seemed just as absorbed in his own thoughts. When Parker unlocked the front door, though, Taylor finally said,

"Do you have some lotion I could use? And maybe some painkillers? My arm is really bothering me."

"Yeah, of course!" Parker replied quickly, then busied himself with getting Taylor water and some Advil first. Then he dug through his bathroom cabinet, unsure of what kind of lotion would be best—he only had a light face moisturizer and a thicker hand cream he used in the winter. He brought them both to Taylor, who had settled on the couch.

"I'm not sure what would be better," he confessed awkwardly, placing both of them on the coffee table. Taylor chuckled, looking them over.

"Probably this one, I think," he said, picking up the tub of cream. He started to pull his arm out of his hoodie, wincing as he moved stiffly.

"Here," Parker said quickly, helping him pull it off. His heart squeezed at the dismayed expression that came across Taylor's face again as he caught sight of his arm. "Do you need help?"

Taylor flinched, shaking his head. "No, it's alright. I got it."

Parker stood there awkwardly for a moment as Taylor started to slather his arm with the lotion, then left to put the unused tube back in his bathroom, taking longer than he needed so Taylor would have some privacy for what felt like a strangely intimate activity.

The whole situation felt so awkward. What was he going to do? They needed to talk, that was for certain, but was now really the best time? But when else would they be spending this much time together without actively doing something else?

"You promised them," he whispered to his reflection in the bathroom mirror, scrubbing a hand through his hair. "Kylie will kick your ass if you don't do it."

It wasn't exactly convincing, but it did strengthen his resolve enough that he finally went back out into the living room where Taylor sat, looking pensively down at his forearm. Already his skin looked a little better, though it was now a bit more pinkish and raw.

"Did that help?" Parker asked softly, sitting down beside him. Taylor mustered a small smile.

"Yeah, a bit," he said, sighing. "I think it's just gonna take a few days to start looking normal again, I guess. Just waiting for the painkillers to kick in."

Parker nodded, then they both sat there silently for a moment. His mind was racing with anticipation. He couldn't chicken out. He had to say it now.

"Could we, um, talk about... About all this?" he said softly, his voice coming out far more timidly than he'd liked. Taylor blinked, glancing up at him in surprise.

"I..." he started, then trailed off. "Yeah. What do you mean?"

"I've been... Thinking about the other day," Parker said resolutely, ignoring how heat rose in his face. "How we... You know, talked about us."

Taylor's expression became pained, and he glanced away. "Yeah, I... I wanted to talk about that too."

Parker hesitated, not expecting Taylor's response. "Oh, uh... Do you want to go first?"

A small smile ghosted across Taylor's lips as he looked at Parker for a long moment, studying his face. Parker's heart started beating faster. He wasn't sure what Taylor was looking for, and was unsure if the other man found it, when he finally leaned back on the sofa and answered, "You first."

Parker nodded. It seemed likely that what they wanted to say was the same, especially after everything that had happened at Taylor's appointment. Despite all the mental rehearsing he'd done, he still had to fight to get the words to come to the forefront of his mind.

"I was thinking about what we talked about," Parker said slowly, trying to keep his gaze trained on Taylor, even though all his instincts told him to look away out of embarrassment. "And I, uh... I changed my mind about wanting to take things slow."

Taylor blinked, blue eyes wide. Parker hesitated, heart thudding painfully in his chest; but then Taylor's expression became more guarded, like he was afraid Parker was going to pull away from whatever they had entirely. So he blurted out,

"I thought that would help make sure I didn't fuck things up, but then I was talking to Kylie and she... I realized I was already fucking things up with you, and I don't want to do that. I want to do this right."

Taylor's mouth dropped open. "You talked to Kylie?"

Parker couldn't hold back the laugh—of all the things Taylor would have latched onto, of course it would be his conversation with Kylie. "Yeah, she, uh... Kind of ambushed me the day I got back from Nashville. I actually had dinner with the rest of the band... She made me think it was something going on with you, and then they had, like... an intervention when I got there. But it's alright. It actually really helped me see how you must have been seeing things, and I realized I've been really stupid."

"I told her not to do that," Taylor groaned, scrubbing a hand through his dirty blond hair and pushing the strands out of his face. "Jesus, I'm sorry, Parker. She really shouldn't have done that."

"No, no, don't apologize," Parker said quickly. "It helped me a lot. I think I needed to hear it from someone else, you know? It made me realize that I, um... I think I felt really, uh, insecure about what you might think of me. Comparing me to Zach. Because he was, you know, this big personality and a fucking rockstar and all that. And I'm just..."

His voice cracked. Taylor's expression became pained, and he was sure the other man understood what he was trying to say, but he needed to say it. If he could admit it to Kylie and the others, then he could be just as vulnerable with Taylor, too.

"I'm just, you know, a regular guy," he said, trying to laugh as he said it, but his eyes were stinging with tears. "I felt like I could never compare to him. And if we weren't together, you would never have to compare us and decide I wasn't... wasn't as good."

"Parker," Taylor murmured, squeezing his hands. "I would never think that. Ever. I never wanted a rockstar. Hell, it was when things started really ramping up with the band that, you know, me and Zach started drifting apart. That was never what was important to me."

"I know. I didn't understand that before, but I see it now," Parker replied, nodding. He gave Taylor's hands a gentle squeeze in response before pulling them away to rub self-consciously at his eyes before continuing. "And, I mean, I was getting so in my head about... About what I *thought* Zach would think about all this, too, that I couldn't think about what it was like for you. Not that I think I could understand what you've gone through, Taylor, because I can't. You're just—so strong and brave, and..."

He clamped his mouth shut, realizing he was rambling, but Taylor was looking at him with a soft, hesitant smile now. So he ventured again,

"All that to say... I'm really sorry about how I handled things when you kissed me, and when we talked afterward. I've just been really, really afraid to mess this up with you. And I think I was trying to find any excuse not to, you know, take things further, so that I wouldn't have to think about... how it was actually me being afraid of losing you. You've been my friend for so long, Taylor, and I would never forgive myself if I messed up our friendship. But I... I've cared about you for so long, too, and I don't think I could hold myself back anymore, either, even if I wanted to."

His voice wavered at the end, and he looked away, embarrassed. After a beat, Taylor's hands clasped his again, warm and soft on his skin. He shot a nervous glance back over at Taylor. The other man had a sympathetic expression, his eyes shining as he met Parker's gaze.

"I understand," he said softly. "Really, I do. But you don't have to worry about losing me as a friend, alright? And... I'm sorry, too. I think neither of us wanted to be the one to... to say it. But I understand why you would have been a lot more hesitant than me. You didn't know about me and Zach, and I know he was your friend, too. And I appreciate how you care about what he would think. God, is it weird that I feel like this would be way easier if he were still here?"

Parker had had the same thought many times himself. If Zach were still here... He probably would have rolled his eyes if Parker had come to him asking what he would think if, hypothetically, he wanted to maybe potentially ask Taylor on a date. He could practically hear Zach's voice telling him to *just fucking go for it.*

"No, I don't think that's weird," Parker laughed faintly. "I think you're right. I think if he could just tell us to our faces we were being dumb, and he didn't care, we might actually believe it."

Taylor laughed. "Yeah, I think you're right."

They both sat there for a long moment, each looking down at their hands clasped between them. There was so much more Parker wanted to say, but Taylor wanted to speak, too, so he held back.

"I, uh," Taylor finally said after a beat, as if he could tell Parker was waiting for him. "I'm... kind of embarrassed about earlier, to be honest. I know how this sounds, but... getting the cast off felt really *final*, I guess. Like he's really... gone. Like everything from then is really over now, you know? I don't know how else to explain it. But I don't want to give you the wrong idea that I'm still sad about him—I mean, I am, but not in a I-wish-he-was-still-here-and-we-were-still-married way. You know?"

The admission made Parker's chest ache with sympathy all over again. His own feelings on the situation were complicated enough, so it was hard to imagine how much more difficult it must have been for Taylor to sort out all his feelings about what had happened. His life had completely changed, and not at all in the way he'd been anticipating and planning for.

"And it doesn't mean I'm not serious about this, about us," Taylor added quickly, uncertainty tinging his voice again. "I mean, it was kind of about Zach, but not really about him either, I guess. I don't know. I don't know how to prove to you I'm not, like, hung up on him still, or just wanting a rebound or—or—"

"Taylor," Parker interrupted, squeezing his hand gently, and the other man clamped his mouth shut immediately. "You don't have to prove anything to me. I believe you. I know it must be complicated. It's complicated for me, too.

Trust me. But that doesn't change how I feel about you, so I believe you that it doesn't change your feelings for me, either."

Taylor's lips quivered. His downturned lashes were damp again, and his eyes were locked onto their clasped hands. He didn't look completely convinced, but Parker hoped that even the tiniest part of Taylor believed him—even a tiny seed of trust now would be enough to bloom with time.

"So what now?" Taylor asked softly after a long moment, looking hesitantly at Parker again. He smiled nervously back, feeling his pulse start to race with nerves once more.

"I want to kiss you again," he said, leaning closer to Taylor. "I want to take you on a real date, something nice, and make it official. I want to do this right."

Taylor's face had split into a smile, but he laughed at that. "That's not what's important to me. Can we just skip past that and be boyfriends?"

Parker laughed, a rush of exhilaration coursing through him. His heart was still pounding with anxiety, but now it was tempered with relief and overwhelming *joy*. Taylor still wanted him, wanted to be his *boyfriend*. The word was like a spark on his tongue. His boyfriend.

"Yes," he said, realizing he hadn't answered Taylor. "Can I kiss you?"

Taylor's smile widened, color rising in his cheeks. "Yes," he answered breathlessly.

Parker closed the distance between them and pressed their lips together. Taylor's mouth was warm and soft, and the faint sound that came from the back of his throat sent heat curling through the pit of Parker's stomach. *His boyfriend.*

One of Taylor's hands came up to cup his cheek, and he tilted his head to press into the contact without breaking their kiss. Taylor's lips curled into a smile against his own, his hand trembling against Parker's skin.

"Your beard is kind of prickly," Taylor murmured when they finally parted, making Parker chuckle.

"I'll shave it if you don't like it," he said quickly. It was hardly a beard, and he alternated between being clean-shaven and scruffy anyway, so if Taylor didn't like the scruff, then he'd gladly shave more frequently.

"No, I like it. I just have to get used to it," Taylor replied, shaking his head before kissing Parker again. "So you'll have to kiss me a lot."

Parker's face ached from smiling. His heart was still beating fast, but this time it was from exhilaration instead of nerves. "I can do that."

He pressed another kiss to Taylor's lips, but when his tongue hesitantly swiped against Parker's lower lip, a sharp knock from the front door made them both jump and pull away, startled.

"Oh, the food," Taylor burst out, as Parker shot a bewildered look over at the door. He held up his phone, which had been face-down on the coffee table in front of them. "I missed the notification. Oops."

The bag of food was sitting neatly in the center of the doormat when Parker opened the door. He carried it inside, his stomach grateful the food had arrived, but his dick very displeased with the interruption. Taylor immediately dug into the chocolate chip waffle when Parker handed it over to him, though, and he felt a small pang of guilt thinking of how he'd rather have gone right back to what they were doing than eat. After a few bites of his own sandwich, though, he decided eating first was the better option.

"How is it?" he asked after Taylor had taken several big, gleeful bites of the waffle, which was smothered in butter and whipped cream and syrup. Just looking at such a total sugar bomb made Parker's teeth hurt, but Taylor smiled over at him in response, something wistful in his expression.

"It's really good," he replied, nodding. "I'm sure it's more us than the waffle, but I really am feeling better already."

Parker laughed, his heart skipping a beat at the way Taylor's eyes sweetly crinkled at the edges, a little smear of whipped cream in the corner of his mouth as he grinned.

"Me too."

Chapter Seventeen
Parker

Once they were done eating, they ended up back on the couch in each other's arms. Parker's heart hadn't slowed at all; Taylor's warm body pressed up against his own sent it racing even faster somehow. For all that they'd talked about, there was so much more he wanted to say.

"Your heart is pounding," Taylor said softly from where his cheek was pressed to Parker's chest, making him laugh self-consciously. "You okay?"

"This feels surreal still, I think," he said. "And... I don't know. I keep thinking about everything. I... I guess I'm nervous about what happens next."

Taylor shifted against him slightly, so he could look up into Parker's face. "What happens next?"

Parker hesitated, squeezing Taylor a little tighter against him, relishing the feel. "Well, first, I wanted to really make this up to you. How I reacted earlier... I still feel really guilty. So I want to help out more to help make it up to you."

Taylor frowned, shaking his head. "You don't have to make anything up to me."

"No, but I want to," Parker replied. "I was thinking I could do all the finishing touches for the Caesura Room you have left, just to get some of that off your plate. I'm not sure exactly how much is left, but anything outside of the permit stuff, I can handle it for you. So if there's anything with the contractors, or just stuff you were waiting to do until after you got your cast off, I'll work on it for you. Okay?"

This time, Taylor laughed, sounding incredulous. "I mean, if you really want to... But, seriously, dude, you don't need to do anything for me. I appreciate all your help so far, of course, but don't feel pressured."

"I know. But I want to. I just want to... to help you, you know? To—to take care of you," Parker stammered, a flush rising in his face at the admission. Taylor's body stiffened in his arms, and for a panicked moment, he thought maybe that was the entirely wrong thing to say—that Taylor didn't need anyone to take care of him, that he'd already overstepped some boundary—but then Taylor squeezed him tighter, leaning closer into him.

"You want to take care of me?" he asked, his voice taking on a husky edge.

"Yes," Parker breathed.

"I want to take care of you," Taylor said, pressing a kiss to Parker's jaw. The way they were laying together, Parker could feel Taylor's cock pressing against his thigh, making his intentions perfectly clear. "Can we... Do you want to...?"

"Yes," Parker repeated, before Taylor could even finish his question. "But, uh, I wasn't really expecting to... I mean, my bed isn't made, so, I don't know, my room is kind of messy, I guess."

Taylor blinked, then laughed. "I don't care. I don't even remember the last time I made my bed. We would just mess up the sheets, anyway." His grin took on a teasing expression. "Hopefully."

"Hopefully," Parker echoed. They untangled from their embrace and stumbled up from the sofa, Taylor following as Parker led the way to the bedroom. It wasn't as messy as he'd feared—no dirty laundry on the floor, and no egregious clutter on his bedside table or the little listening nook by the window where his smaller record player stood. Still, his bed was unmade, and he wasn't sure when he'd last vacuumed.

He couldn't even exactly remember the last time he'd had anyone at all in his room—had it really been that long? Maybe he should have expected this. After all, he'd wanted to talk to Taylor about everything today, had hoped that they would maybe *finally* make things official, so why hadn't he considered that it all could lead to this?

He was spiraling again. Parker paused and took in a long, slow breath, trying to steady his nerves. He had imagined what it would be like to have sex with Taylor on and off for the better part of a decade; now it seemed like it was going to happen, and the last thing he wanted was to freak out and ruin it for both of them.

"Hey," Taylor said softly, coming up behind him to wrap his arms around Parker's waist. Parker let out the deep breath he'd been holding in, leaning back a little into Taylor's arms. The contact instantly helped quiet his mind, soothing away the worry. It was easier not to overthink these things when Taylor was right there with him. "Don't be nervous, alright?"

Parker laughed faintly. "Too late for that. But this helps." Taylor's mouth ghosted against the back of his neck, pressing feather-light kisses that sent surges of electric sensation through his nerves. His right arm still moved hesitantly, but Parker laced his fingers with Taylor's left hand instead, pulling him forward until they were both sinking onto the bed.

"So, I, uh... I mean, do you want to top?" Parker asked, heat rising in his face again as he stumbled through the question. "We can go either way, or if you wanted something else... Whatever you want."

Taylor chuckled, nestling closer to him. "I just said don't be so nervous."

Parker winced. "Right. Sorry."

"If you don't have a preference," Taylor continued slowly, thinking it over. "I think I want you to top me."

A rush of heat and desire went straight to Parker's cock—he would have been happy with whatever Taylor wanted, but hearing Taylor say it filled him with a sudden boldness. He quickly pushed himself up so he was over Taylor. The other man steadily met his gaze, blue eyes wide at first with surprise, then filling with a warm glow as he smiled.

"Okay," Parker replied in a rush. "Yeah. I can do that. I guess we should probably get undressed first, though, huh?"

Taylor laughed, nodding. Parker helped him pull his shirt off, still moving gingerly around his right arm, then leaned back so Taylor could pull his jeans off. He was wearing a pair of boxer briefs that were a sweet peachy orange-pink color, but Parker's eyes were fixed on the bulge of his cock underneath. He knew what he wanted then, before getting lube or condoms or anything else—he *needed* Taylor's cock in his mouth.

Taylor shifted slightly, legs closing together shyly as he laughed. "Come on, dude. Don't act like you've never seen one before."

Parker realized he was still wearing all his clothes, and he'd been staring very pointedly at Taylor's underwear—he shook himself into action, despite the burning warmth in his face.

"S-Sorry," he stammered, pulling his own shirt off hastily. "I just—I just—"

Taylor's gaze had softened when Parker could see again. "I'm just teasing. It's okay. I, uh... I like it. Look all you want."

Parker's cock bucked eagerly in pants, and he took a moment to give Taylor a longer, closer look. The other man had been tall and lean for as long as Parker had known him; he'd been skinnier in college, then a little more athletic before the band took off. He was lean now, with less definition to his muscles in the time he'd had to take it easy since the accident.

Taylor let his legs fall open a little more again, but Parker tore his eyes away before they could linger too long on his underwear again. He'd get to it soon enough. Instead, he kicked off his own pants, grateful he'd chosen a pair of black briefs today that were more comfortable with the skinny jeans he'd been wearing, rather than the baggy boxers he might have picked if he'd gone with looser pants. He was sure his erection was just as obvious under the dark fabric; the thought of Taylor looking at it, eyeing him as hungrily as he was drinking in Taylor now, only made him harder.

He wedged one leg between Taylor's as he settled back over the other man, pressing a kiss to the bare skin of his collarbone. Taylor let out a faint sound that was almost a moan, turning his head to expose more of the sensitive skin of his neck. Parker traveled lower, feeling Taylor shiver under him as his lips skimmed over his sternum, his ribs, the softest part of his stomach, the divot of his hipbone, until finally the waistband of his underwear made him pause.

"Can I...?" he asked, looking up at Taylor. The other man's face was flushed, and his eyes were dark with desire—he looked utterly undone as he nodded quickly, before Parker could even finish the question.

"Yes please," he rasped. Parker didn't have to be told twice; he pulled down the waistband of Taylor's underwear and drank in the sight of his hard cock, precum glistening at the tip. He hesitated for a beat, then reached down to pull off his own underwear, not wanting Taylor to be the only one naked. He could feel Taylor's eyes on his body. For a moment, they were both completely still, each taking in the sight of the other.

Taylor's body was so... perfectly, wonderfully *normal*. He'd spent so long pining after Taylor—getting caught up in the band's sudden rise to fame and his own preconceived notions of what the other man might be like—that he almost hadn't known what to expect. But here, naked in Parker's bed, Taylor wasn't some cherubic angel of music, or a pornographic rockstar.

He was just Taylor, and that was better than anything Parker could have imagined. His heart skipped a beat. *This* was what was real. Taylor wasn't a daydream any longer, but a real, living, breathing human man, warm and solid beneath him. What had Parker ever been so afraid of?

He dipped his head back down to kiss against Taylor's hipbone again, then pressing lower to where it became his thigh. He couldn't hold back—the kiss became biting as he pressed his teeth to the sensitive flesh, then swiped his tongue over the same spot. Taylor hissed, but didn't pull away. Parker kissed the tender skin along the crease of Taylor's thigh, spreading his legs open, then finally licked a long, measured stripe up the underside of Taylor's cock. Heat and salt burst along his tongue, but his senses were overpowered by the low, needy moan that Taylor made in response.

His mouth closed over the head of Taylor's cock, making him gasp and shudder.

"Fuck, Parker," Taylor panted, his hands gripping desperately at Parker's bedsheets. "I didn't—I wasn't—Fuck, I wasn't expecting *this*."

Parker let out a soft hum of a laugh, but continued to take more and more of Taylor's cock into his mouth in slow, measured movements—relishing in every little moan and whimper he got out of Taylor in the process. One of Taylor's hands finally settled on his head, fingers lacing through his short, dark hair. His hips rocked, pushing his cock further into Parker's mouth, making him moan.

"Parker," Taylor panted, his voice ragged. His fingers tightened in Parker's hair, pulling him away. "Hold on, hold on."

Parker let Taylor pull him up. "Too much?"

Taylor's face was flushed pink as he nodded. "It just... felt really good. And I didn't want to cum yet. So..."

Parker's cock bucked eagerly at the thought of making Taylor cum. "Still want me on top?"

Taylor nodded quickly, a small, nervous smile playing at his lips. "Yeah."

His fingers had relaxed their grip in Parker's hair, so he dipped his head back down to kiss the soft skin just below his belly button, making Taylor laugh. He kissed and licked lower again, this time moving past Taylor's cock, pushing his hips up—Taylor stifled a small gasp as Parker gently pressed his teeth against the fleshy part of his ass cheek. He let out a small laugh at the sensation, only for it to morph into a moan when Parker replaced his teeth with his tongue, working toward the center of him.

He pulled back so he could see better, then used his hands to gently spread Taylor's cheeks apart. The little puckered divot of his asshole was the same dusky pink as the flushed head of his cock.

"Fuck, you have such a pretty little hole," Parker heard himself say. Mortification burned in his face—the words were completely unconscious—but the soft, needy sound Taylor made in response, and the way his cock twitched between his legs, made him think maybe it was the right thing to say, anyway.

"Jesus, Parker," Taylor whimpered, covering his face with one hand.

"You do," Parker said, spurred on by his reaction. He shifted his hands so he could swipe his thumb lightly over the sensitive flesh, tracing lazy circles around it. "Hand me the lube."

Taylor didn't respond, only moved his hands frantically around him to find the small tube—it had slipped under a pillow—then shoved it into Parker's outstretched hand.

Parker uncapped it and let some of the slick liquid drip in a steady stream down onto Taylor's exposed hole, making the other man hiss at the sensation. With his other hand, he rubbed the lube onto Taylor's skin and his fingers. When he was done, he set the lube back down, wrapped one hand around Taylor's cock, and with the other, pressed a finger against his hole. Taylor made a faint sound that wasn't quite a moan, but the first finger slipped in easily.

"Fuck," Taylor panted, squirming underneath Parker. "It's—It's been a little while, so go slow, okay?"

"I will," Parker said, nodding. "I just want to make you feel good."

Taylor bit back a laugh. "It feels good."

"Tell me if it's too much," Parker said, and Taylor nodded. He worked Taylor open as slowly and gently as he could, moving just the one finger into him carefully until there was hardly any resistance at all. The second slid in alongside the first just as easily; Taylor made another soft, slightly uncomfortable noise, so Parker waited before moving again. After a beat, Taylor nodded encouragingly, and he kept going.

"Good?" Parker asked, and Taylor nodded again. Each drag of his fingers made the flesh within feel a little softer around him, a little less tight. God, he was going to feel so fucking good around Parker's cock.

He moved a bit faster now, slowly ramping up until he was sure he could push a third finger inside. But he was relishing how Taylor's face was flushed, the way his eyes were dark with desire, the way his breath stuttered and caught as Parker prepped him.

"Ready for one more?" Parker asked softly, and Taylor nodded, eyes squeezing closed. "I think you're almost ready for my cock, aren't you?"

Taylor bit his lip, nodding again. "I like this. I like you talking dirty."

Parker flushed, nervous now that Taylor had mentioned it, but he forced himself to reply. "Yeah?"

"Tell me more."

"You look so hot like this," Parker said, eyes roaming up and down Taylor's body. "Naked and so tight around me in my bed. Look how easily you're taking a third finger. Your cute little hole is so greedy. It just wants my cock, doesn't it?"

Taylor whimpered, nodding. He reached one hand down between his legs, searching for where Parker's fingers entered his body, feeling the slick friction. Parker grabbed Taylor's hand and guided it to his own cock. "Feel how hard I am for you?"

Taylor's long fingers encircled and stroked him, making him moan.

"You're so big," Taylor panted, squeezing him. "You're gonna feel so good inside me."

Parker rocked his hips, pushing his cock through the slick pressure of Taylor's fist—it felt good, but he knew Taylor's hole would feel a thousand times better.

"I'm ready," Taylor urged him. "Come on."

"Okay," Parker laughed. "Hold on." With his free hand, he found the condom he'd placed on the bedside drawer, ripped the wrapper open with his teeth, and rolled it on. Then he gently pulled his fingers from Taylor's body and pressed the head of his cock to his soft, pliant hole.

"Ready for me?" Parker asked.

"Yes, come *on*," Taylor said, even more urgency in his voice this time. Parker didn't need any more encouragement; he pushed his hips forward, and Taylor's hole all but sucked him in. He moaned at the heat and pressure enveloping his cock, and Taylor let out a soft sound that was just as relieved, just as needy.

"Gentle," he panted again, and Parker nodded. He moved unbearably slowly, every nerve in his body crying for relief. He'd imagined this moment so many times before, and more than anything, he wanted to make Taylor feel good, wanted to see him come apart with pleasure.

He groaned when he felt the back of Taylor's thighs press against his pelvis; he was buried to the base of his cock. Taylor's chest heaved as he panted, eyes closed. His left hand had a vice grip on Parker's sheets, but the other hand was loosely curled around his cock.

"Go on," Parker urged. Taylor's eyes flickered open. "I want to see you jerk yourself off while I fuck you."

Taylor's insides clenched around him, his cock bucking; Parker had to fight to stop himself from laughing with delight. He didn't think he'd ever been quite this domineering before, but he'd never been with anyone who seemed to like it this much, either.

"I—Okay," Taylor panted, and he started to stroke his cock in slow, languid movements. Parker moved his hips at the same pace, pulling out until he felt the tight ring of muscle squeezing the head of his cock, then pushing all the way in again. Taylor moaned, pressing his free hand to his mouth to stifle the sound. Parker wanted to tell him not to—he wanted to hear every noise Taylor made—but he thought if he did, he might cum far too soon.

Everything in him felt *right*. Like his head was buzzing, but instead of all the usual thoughts about the future and worry about how this would turn out, it was full of comfortable silence. Like his brain could finally let go of it all, and all his focus was on Taylor, making Taylor feel good.

He wanted to kiss Taylor—wanted to feel Taylor pant and gasp against his mouth as he came. Parker shifted positions so he was right on top of Taylor, their chests pressed together. Taylor let out a soft, surprised noise that Parker stifled with his lips—then he moaned, pressing his tongue into Parker's mouth.

Taylor's free hand was in Parker's hair again, but rather than gripping his hair, he was scratching his scalp in a soothing rhythm.

"You feel so good," Parker groaned when they parted, their noses still brushing. He was moving faster now, his hips moving of their own accord. Every nerve in his body was alight, hyper aware of Taylor's body against him, around him.

"I'm close," Taylor breathed—Parker could still feel him touching himself between their bodies. "Fuck, you're—you're gonna make me cum."

Parker bit his lip, the words pushing him right up to the edge himself. He just had to hold back until Taylor came, just a little longer—

"Let me feel you," he urged, his words coming out as a breathless whisper. "I want to feel it—want to feel you cum around my cock."

Taylor's hand stilled as he cried out, shuddering around Parker as he came, squeezing Parker's cock even tighter. Parker moaned, following him over the edge.

Everything in him burned with heat and light. Taylor's skin against him, Taylor's scent in his nose, the warmth of Taylor's cum caught between their bellies, the heat of his core so tight around Parker's cock—it was all utter bliss. It was all *right*. How had he ever been so afraid of messing things up? How could it have ever been anything but perfect, just like this?

Taylor's fingers stroking his hair guided him back into his body. His face was pressed into the crook of Taylor's shoulder, and he pressed soft, tired kisses to his sweat-damp skin, making Taylor shiver.

"You okay?" he asked, propping himself up. Taylor met his gaze. His face was still flushed, and his eyelashes glistened with tears, but the sweetly satisfied smile on his lips was reassurance enough for Parker.

"Yeah," Taylor replied softly, cupping Parker's face and pulling him in for a kiss. "Are you?"

Parker closed his eyes, leaning into the soft contact. He didn't think he'd ever been more okay, more happy, in his whole life.

"Yeah," he said, opening his eyes again. Taylor's eyes were blue and shining, like the sky after rain. "I'm good."

Chapter Eighteen
Parker

THREE MONTHS LATER

Get Well Soon to Play Final Farewell Show at New San Diego
Venue, Proceeds Going to Charity

Punk News Net, March 9

by Parker Flores

Over six months since the unexpected death of lead
singer Zach Ross, Get Well Soon is playing their final show
in their hometown of San Diego, CA.

The show marks the grand opening of the new venue,
The Caesura Room, owned and operated by the band's
keyboardist Taylor Lewis-Ross.

The Caesura Room aims to become the premier location
for indie musicians in southern California, with a special
focus on LGBTQ+ performers. At the time of Ross' death,
he and Lewis-Ross had been married for six years,

making them among the first gay couples to achieve their significant success in the world of rock music.

"In musical notation, a caesura is a type of rest, a break between stanzas or between sections of a piece," Lewis-Ross said about the new venue. "That's what my goal is in opening this new venue. That it can be a place where LGBTQ+ musicians of all genres can come get a break from the rest of the world, from other venues that might not be so understanding of their identities. Cultivating a fanbase that was safe and inclusive was one of the most important things to Zach. Get Well Soon might be disbanding, but this is my way of carrying on that mission."

The proceeds of this charity show will be evenly split between charities selected by the band, including the local LGBTQ+ Resource Center and Chords for Kids, a nonprofit which supports music programs in schools.

Tickets to the venue are sold out, but digital tickets to view the show via livestream are available on the band's website.

/ /

After all of Parker's hard work putting the finishing touches on the venue—just as he'd promised Taylor he would—the day of the show had finally arrived. It was a bittersweet feeling, though Parker was sure his feelings about it were not nearly as conflicted as Taylor's, who had been quieter than usual all day leading up to the show. Parker had arrived at the Caesura Room during sound check and had watched Taylor and the others play their warm-up song on stage; since then, he'd been wound up as tight as a guitar string. It was understandable, of course, and it meant that he was mostly glued to Parker's hip, so he couldn't complain.

The venue was packed, spectators squeezed all the way up to the barricade. The opening act was downstairs, getting ready to get on stage in just a few minutes—Parker, Taylor, and the rest of the band were upstairs in the green room, looking down on the stage from the little window. There were snacks and drinks on the table, but Taylor hadn't touched them; he'd been sitting pressed right up next to Parker since they'd sat down, one knee bouncing nervously.

Parker squeezed his hand for what must have been the hundredth time, smiling encouragingly at him. "Everything's going to be great."

Taylor grimaced, pressing his free hand down on his thigh, as if to hold his bouncy leg in place. "I know, you're right. I'm just nervous."

Parker pressed a soft kiss to his forehead, and Taylor leaned into the contact. The one benefit of Taylor being nervous was how cuddly he became. Parker didn't think he would ever get tired of holding the other man in his arms, so this just gave him more of an excuse to hold his hand or wrap an arm around his waist.

"Thank you again for doing all this," Taylor said softly, his voice partly muffled by how he'd rested his head against Parker's shoulder. "I know I've said it already, but... I don't know how I could have done this without you."

Parker beamed, hugging Taylor a little tighter. "I loved doing it. Honestly, the hardest part was figuring out all the livestreaming stuff for the show tonight. Thank God Jasper knows about this kind of thing. I'm way too old to make sense of it."

Taylor chuckled. He'd been the one who had suggested the livestream, knowing the Caesura Room was small, and only so many people could physically be there. But Parker's expertise only extended as far as operating his website and posting his podcast online. They were lucky their new sound tech, Jasper, knew how to set it all up. Thanks to the livestream option, they'd sold nearly ten times as many digital tickets as they did in-person tickets—a figure which still baffled Parker, but barely seemed to phase Taylor. It was no stadium tour, but was still pretty significant as far as Parker was concerned.

"Thanks for working with all my unrealistic demands," Taylor teased, leaning closer to him. Parker laughed, warmth bubbling up in his chest at the contact.

"It's not all altruistic," Parker replied. "I had to impress you so I can keep working out of the venue for as long as you'll let me. Lots of shows to write about and all that."

He felt Taylor smile. "Hopefully you'll be around forever," he replied softly.

Parker's heart skipped a beat, but before he could formulate a reply, a cheer rose up from the crowd, the lights dimming. The opening act was about to start, which meant Get Well Soon would be going on in less than an hour. Taylor leaned closer to the window—the other side was covered with privacy film, so they could see clearly through it, but the audience outside couldn't see them—to watch as the group took the stage.

"I just had the thought that I probably won't be watching many more shows from up here," Taylor said softly, just loud enough for Parker to hear over the growly guitar chords that had started up. "All the other bands will be in the green room... I'll probably watch from the bar, or backstage, or just listen from the box office."

"I guess that's true," Parker replied. "Better enjoy it while it lasts then, huh?"

"*So* sorry to interrupt," Kylie's voice came from behind them. "But Moss just sent up some of the signature cocktails for us to have before the show. Let's have a toast!" She grinned widely as they turned to face her; even though it had been almost three months, she still got the same self-satisfied expression seeing them together, as if it were an accomplishment that she was solely responsible for.

"Have you tried it yet?" Taylor asked, extricating himself from Parker's arms. "Moss and I spent a while working on it. I had to re-learn how different liquors tasted."

"Ooh, I haven't tried it! I didn't realize you worked on it. I figured it was all Moss' creation," Kylie chirped, turning her attention back to the tray of drinks on the table where she and the rest of the band had been sitting.

She and Taylor talked about the drink to each other for a long moment; Parker hung back a few steps and watched, unsure if he should join for what seemed to be the band's last hurrah. Taylor and Kylie had their backs to him now; from the opposite side of the table, Angie caught his eye and smiled brightly at him. He smiled back, even when Dean glanced up at him, then looked back down at the tray of drinks with barely an acknowledgment. They had said polite hellos earlier, but that was all. He was still standoffish with Parker; but Taylor had assured him that things were fine between them now, so he didn't really care.

Taylor reached out for him, shaking him from his rumination. Parker stepped closer, and Taylor wrapped one arm around his waist, lifting up his drink with the other. "I, uh, I don't really know what to say," he chuckled, making the others laugh. "Zach was always better at this than me. But, well, I guess, thank you for doing this and coming along for the ride since the beginning. I'm so thankful to have you all in my life. This may be our last show, but you guys will always be family to me."

"Aw, Taylor, don't make me tear up. This mascara is only so waterproof," Angie said, fanning her eyes with one hand. "I feel the same way. No matter what we do after this, Get Well Soon is always gonna feel like home to me, you know?"

"I think Zach would be pretty proud of us now," Dean said softly. Angie blinked harder against the tears that were visibly welling in her eyes as she reached over to squeeze her brother's wrist. "We had a pretty incredible run, all things considered, didn't we?"

"We sure did," Kylie agreed, smiling pensively down at the drink she swirled in her hand. "Who would've thought things would end up like this when we were just a bunch of college dropouts playing in a garage every day?"

"That was all Zach," Taylor agreed, chuckling. He leaned closer to Parker. "Well... Cheers, everyone."

"Get Well Soon!" Kylie exclaimed, lifting her drink, and everyone echoed the cheer, including Parker. They clinked their glasses together and took a long drink. The signature cocktail was sort of like an amaretto sour, Parker thought as he drank it, sweet and tangy all at once. It wasn't something he would have typically ordered for himself, but it tasted good.

"Ooh, Taylor, that's *fire*," Angie exclaimed, slamming her empty glass down. "You said you made this drink?"

"Me and Moss," Taylor laughed, shaking his head. "They did most of the work. I just taste tested and gave the final approval. It doesn't even have a name yet."

They stood chatting around the table until the sound from the stage finally faded out and the lights brightened back up. Taylor glanced up at Parker as the silence filled the room.

When he was nervous, it was Parker he looked for. The thought made him smile; Taylor smiled back, although there was still some tension in his brow. Parker leaned over and kissed his forehead.

"You got this," he said softly. "You guys are gonna be great."

Taylor nodded, but couldn't seem to bring himself to respond. Instead, he leaned closer to Parker, hugging him. Parker wrapped his arms around him, holding him tightly. "It's gonna be great," he continued in a low murmur, his lips just ghosting against Taylor's hair. "You're going to do so well. And then you'll never have to worry about it again."

"Ugh, get a room," Kylie teased, before reaching over and squeezing Taylor's upper arm. "We've got this, dude. It's a show just like any other."

Taylor mumbled something that was lost against Parker's chest, then turned his head to say to her, "I know. I just feel..." He trailed off, then looked back up at Parker sheepishly. "I'm not normally this nervous before a show, I swear."

Parker's gaze softened. "I understand."

A sharp knock rapped at the green room door, then it swung open. The stage manager bustled into the room; Kylie squealed with delight when she saw him. He was wearing a dark sport jacket over what looked like a silky cheetah print button down, a black feather boa, and a tiny tiara that was somehow affixed to his short blonde hair.

"Oh my god, *Reid*," Taylor exclaimed, pulling away from Parker to stifle a laugh. "What, uh, what's going on?"

"What? You thought I wasn't going to celebrate our very first show?" Reid replied in a mockingly haughty tone. He grinned and twirled in a circle, the ends of the boa fluttering out with the movement. "Don't get used to it, babes. I only bust these out for special occasions. Well, the shirt's in my normal rotation, but you get the idea."

"You look amazing," Kylie said, laughing.

"Oh, I know," Reid replied with a wink. "Alright, alright, I came here on business. The stage crew has everything set up for you guys, so start heading backstage now, please. By the way, Dean, your friend got here about ten minutes ago, and I had him wait backstage."

"Sweet," Dean replied simply, shooting Reid a thumbs-up. Parker's stomach did a flip-flop; he'd known Rogelio would be here, but knowing they would be together backstage while the band was performing... It wasn't like he would be obligated to say anything to the other man, but with their admittedly distant connection, it would feel too weird to treat him like a stranger.

"Parker, hands off my performer," Reid said, interrupting his thoughts as the other man approached, lightly swatting the arm still wrapped around Taylor's waist. "He might be your boyfriend and my manager, but right now he's *also* my talent, and the last thing I need is you clinging to him down these stairs and making him trip. I swear, this staircase is going to cause a lawsuit at some point."

Parker laughed, giving Taylor's hip one last squeeze before releasing him. "Alright, alright. He's all yours."

"Do you really think the stairs are that bad?" Taylor said nervously as they headed for the door, Reid ushering them through. "I mean, they're a little narrow, but..."

"At the moment? No," Reid replied, carefully closing the green room door behind him. "But if someone up here has been drinking, and it's been a year so the hand rail's wobbly? Who can say?"

"Don't worry about it now," Parker added. Taylor frowned, eyeing the handrail as they walked down the stairs. Reid made a tutting sound from behind him.

"Ugh, you're right. Sorry, boss," Reid said. "Didn't mean to put anything on your manager plate right now. Forget I said anything and break a leg, alright? I'll see you after the show."

Before Taylor could respond, Reid was already bustling away. Parker and Taylor exchanged a look, then Taylor laughed, shrugging. They turned the corner to head backstage.

The girls were standing near the curtain, cautiously peeking out at the crowd, smiling and talking amongst themselves; a little further back, Dean was standing with a taller man who looked nervous and out-of-place. His black hair was slicked back at the top with a fresh fade, piercings in his ears and nose, wearing a leather jacket over a plain white shirt, a silver chain necklace, and dark jeans over black boots.

It had to be Rogelio. Dean and the other man were talking, and Parker definitely didn't want to interrupt. But Rogelio's eyes flickered over Dean's shoulder toward them—they landed briefly on Taylor, then Parker. Then he looked back at Dean quickly, his expression stoic.

He could introduce himself later, maybe. If he even wanted to talk to him. Right now, Parker only cared about Taylor, who would be going onstage any minute.

"Taylor," he said, before the other man could step away from him. Taylor paused, turning to face Parker; his expression morphed into surprise, and a flush rose in his cheeks. Parker grabbed both his hands, holding them tightly. "I know you're nervous, and nothing I say will really make that go away, but I just want you to know that I'm really excited to see you perform, and I know it's going to be amazing. You're one of the most incredible people I've ever met, and you're an amazing musician. You've been doing this for years, you have it down to an art. Everyone out there is rooting for you. Everyone out there believes in you. And I believe in you, too."

Taylor's face reddened, and for a beat, Parker worried he had only embarrassed Taylor or made him more anxious—then Taylor's lip quivered as he tried to respond, his mouth working silently, before he finally managed to speak.

"I, uh… I think that's the nicest thing anyone's ever said to me," he stammered, barely able to meet Parker's eyes with a sweetly flustered expression. "Thanks, Parker. That really means a lot to me. And it does help."

Parker cupped Taylor's face in his hands, closed the space between them, and kissed him. He could feel Taylor's pulse fluttering rapidly where his fingers brushed against the other man's neck, but Taylor kissed him back fiercely, desperately—his hands clutched tight to the front of Parker's shirt. Even now, though they had been official for a few months, it still didn't feel quite real that he could just kiss Taylor after so many years of longing. Taylor had to be onstage any minute, but he couldn't bring himself to keep the kiss short and chaste, especially with how Taylor was clinging to him.

When they finally parted, Taylor's eyes were bright. He looked silently at Parker for a long moment, a small smile on his face. Parker still held Taylor's face in his hands, lightly brushing his thumb over the other man's cheekbones. Even in the dim lighting backstage, he could see there was still a blush in his cheeks.

"Thank you," Taylor finally said, his voice coming out just loud enough for Parker to hear. "I think I'll be okay now."

Parker smiled, stifling a laugh, then kissed him again, more gently this time on his forehead. "Good. Break a leg and all that. I think they're waiting for you."

Behind them, looking politely away, the other three band members had congregated along with a member of the stage crew. Taylor turned to look over his shoulder, and Parker let his hands finally fall away. They weren't quite ready to go onstage, but it would be any moment now, judging from how the crew member kept peeking out toward the stage and checking his watch.

"Parker, I..." Taylor started, looking back at him. He looked somehow flustered and resolute all at once with determination brightening his eyes, but a heady flush still on his face. "I mean... Thank you. Really. You should give pep talks more often."

Parker let himself laugh aloud this time, shaking his head. "I'll keep that in mind. Now go on!"

Taylor nodded, still smiling, as he turned to join the rest of the band. Parker looked back over to see Rogelio still standing in the same spot, his hands shoved in his pockets. Despite the casual air that he was so obviously trying to project, the man looked small and alone, the crew giving him a wide berth as they bustled by.

A pang of sympathy rose in Parker's chest. All things considered, Rogelio had been dealt a pretty shitty hand in all this too. Taylor had decided that the knowledge of his and Zach's separation would stay between the band and their families—and Parker and Rogelio, of course. But it made Parker wonder if Rogelio had anyone to talk to about all this, or if respecting Taylor's wishes meant he couldn't tell anyone else about his boyfriend dying. How many people in Rogelio's life even knew about Zach and what had happened?

He had been debating between introducing himself to Rogelio, or just politely ignoring the other man for the duration of the show, but the thought tipped him over the edge. He glanced briefly over at Taylor and the band, who were now talking amongst themselves, before steeling himself and striding over to Rogelio.

"Hey," he said, stepping alongside him. "I'm Parker."

He offered his hand. Rogelio looked at him uncertainly for a beat, his eyes flickering down to Parker's outstretched hand. Then he reached over to shake it. "I'm Rogelio. You're, uh, with Taylor, right?"

"Yeah," Parker agreed; despite the strange circumstances of their meeting, hearing the other man acknowledge that he was *with* Taylor sent a sweet thrill through his chest. God, he hoped they weren't so obviously, obnoxiously obsessed with each other as it felt sometimes. "Nice to meet you. Taylor told me about, uh... How he knows you. So I figured I'd come introduce myself."

Rogelio nodded, but his expression was still guarded. He didn't say anything, so Parker continued uncertainly, "I guess I wanted to say, uh, I'm sorry for your loss. Zach was... Well, he made a big impact on a lot of people, obviously. Zach and I were friends, too, so... I guess what I'm trying to say is that this all seems like a crappy situation and I'm, um, open to being friends if you ever want to talk."

Rogelio's expression had softened somewhat, though he still looked mostly skeptical. "Sure. Thanks."

"No problem," Parker replied, glancing away awkwardly. Maybe he was overstepping—clearly Rogelio didn't want to be friends, and maybe he'd made an assumption about the other man not having anyone to talk to. He'd been trying to be nice, but...

Rogelio snorted. He was stifling a smirk, but met Parker's eyes now as he shot him a confused look. "Sorry. It's just you seem nicer than Dean made you out to be. Not sure why I'm surprised, though. He kind of hates everyone."

Surprised, Parker could only stare at him for a moment. Then a relieved chuckle escaped him, and he managed to reply, "You know, I've always felt like Dean hated me for no reason. Glad I'm not the only one who noticed."

"It's just the way he is, to be honest," Rogelio agreed, shaking his head. His gaze was fixed over at the band, where they were still huddled together—it looked like a member of the stage crew was giving them a final briefing, so none of them were paying attention to Parker and Rogelio. "Thanks for that. I appreciate it, really. It's definitely a... weird situation to be in. Zach and I had only been seeing each other for a few months, but... I don't know. I liked him a lot. I think things could have gotten serious with him, you know? So... It's a strange place to be."

"That makes sense," Parker agreed. "He was a good guy. It sucks that everything worked out like this."

"Do you think it's weird that I'm here?" Rogelio asked abruptly. "Like, is it weird if I keep coming to shows here? I swear I'm not, like, trying to stalk Taylor or anything... I'm just local, and there aren't a lot of venues like this. And it does kind of... make me feel closer to Zach, in a way, I guess. You would know better than Dean, I think. Would Taylor be upset if I come around sometimes?"

"Not at all," Parker replied quickly. The question had taken him aback, but from everything Taylor had said about Rogelio, it was clear that the only feelings Taylor had toward him were positive, even compassionate. Even through his surprise, Parker was sure Rogelio's presence wouldn't bother Taylor at all. "In fact, I think it would make him happy to know he could help. So don't feel like you have to stay away, okay?"

Rogelio's brows furrowed, and he glanced away self-consciously, as if he didn't quite believe Parker. "That's, uh... That's a relief. Thank you."

Parker would have added more, but then the lights from the stage started to dim, and a cheer rose up from the crowd that was nearly deafening, even backstage.

"C'mon," Parker said, grinning in anticipation. Rogelio followed him as they took up the spot where the band had been standing just a moment ago. From there they had a clear view of the stage: Dean settling into his seat behind the drum set, Angie and Kylie standing on opposite ends of the stage, Taylor partly between them at the keyboard, and at the front of the stage, the empty mic for Zach.

Taylor's eyes flickered back toward him, the noise of the guitars and cymbals starting up. Parker gave Taylor as encouraging of a smile as he could muster, and after a beat, the other man returned the smile. Then Taylor took in a deep breath with his eyes closed—Parker could practically see the transformation settle over him—and turned back to the crowd screaming for his attention.

Chapter Nineteen
Taylor

"Hello, San Diego," Taylor said into his mic, and a resounding, unintelligible roar answered him. His heart was thudding so hard in his chest, it was nearly all he could hear—so loud he was sure the mic could pick up the rapid thrum of it. His fingers trembled above the keyboard. But the same quiet calm had settled over him now that he was onstage as it always had, as if his body still felt the anxiety that had been churning in his stomach just moments before, but his mind was no longer aware of it.

He looked out toward the crowd, but his eyes snagged on the empty mic at the front of the stage. It wasn't plugged in, purely symbolic; the band had placed a small picture of Zach in front of it. Now, it was surrounded with all sorts of little trinkets: guitar picks; CDs and vinyls; flowers and candles and rosaries; envelopes and other folded-up pieces of paper. Everyone in the venue had transformed the mic into a shrine.

He could so clearly see into the eyes of the people in the front row, their varying expressions of excitement and grief. He'd almost forgotten what it was like, how intimate a show in a small venue like this could be.

"Thank you so much for being here tonight," he continued, looking back down at his hands. The sight of it all filled his chest with... something. He still couldn't quite name the jumble of mixed feelings that the memory of Zach elicited. "We're Get Well Soon, and this is our very last show."

They launched into the first song amid the screams and cheers that arose. Everyone sang together in place of Zach, and the audience sang along, their collective voices creating a wave that could carry him through the rest of the show. He would be alright.

Despite his months being in the cast, and the weeks in physical therapy, his muscle memory had persisted; after a few practice sessions, he could play the keyboard just as easily as he had before. He barely had to think about it. He'd been so scared that he'd never play again, and now here he was.

The first song passed by in a blur. He and the rest of the band had agreed that they would each have the chance to speak to the crowd individually, so once the last chords faded away, Kylie spoke into her mic.

"We really appreciate each one of you who's here tonight, in person or watching online," she said, lightly strumming her bass. "Whether you've been a fan for a day, or a decade, you're all part of our journey. We couldn't have done this without you. And I know Zach would be so stoked that you're here tonight, too. Being here in front of you guys, singing his heart out, was his favorite thing in the whole world. So thanks for helping us keep his memory alive tonight."

Cheers and cries rose up from the audience as they went into the next song. It had been a challenge to create the setlist for tonight, knowing it was the last time any of these songs would be heard live. At first, Taylor had been worried the list was too long, but now he worried it would all go by too quickly. They had picked all the fan favorites, along with their own personal preferences, but would it be enough? Surely, someone out there was going to be disappointed that they didn't hear their favorite song one last time.

Luckily, it was easy to push the worries from his mind when he was playing and singing with the rest of the band. Being on tour was exhausting, but performing like this, being on stage—that had always been where he felt the most at peace—all his worries drowned out by the music. He barely had to think about what he was doing, and the words came easily, even though he wasn't the best singer.

They went through a few more songs before Angie spoke. Her voice was shaky, and Taylor could tell she was holding back tears.

"I'm going to be thankful for the rest of my life that I got to be part of all this," she said, her guitar echoing softly. "Seeing Zach's passion for music, and being able to be part of the band with him, is something that changed my life forever. Thank you all for being here. Thanks for coming on this journey with us. We couldn't have done it without you."

She paused, turning away from her mic to wipe at her eyes, as the crowd responded with noises of sympathy.

"We love you!" a woman's voice cried out, making Angie laugh as she sniffled.

"We love you too!" she replied, then nodded as she met Dean's eyes. He smacked his drumsticks together—*one, two, three, four*—and they went into the next song, the crowd cheering and shouting. They went through a few more songs before it was Dean's turn to speak.

"We miss you, Zach," he said, and the crowd roared in agreement. Taylor knew whatever he was going to say would be short, but he remained silent for longer than expected, the crowd filling his silence with cries of, "Zach! Zach!" and "We love you guys!"

One man near the front shouted out, "Play Wish We Were There!" That finally got Dean to speak again; he let out a humorless huff of a laugh.

"Patience, dude," he said. "Don't act like someone up front hasn't already taken a picture of the set list and posted it online."

The audience laughed in response, various cheers rising up again. Taylor glanced down at the set list taped down to the stage closest to him—were they really more than halfway through it already? There were only a handful of songs left before the encore, then it would all be... over.

His heart pounded so loudly in his ears that he couldn't make out whatever it was that Dean said next. Taylor turned away from his mic, hoping his suddenly rapid breath wasn't being picked up. It was so close to being over, and this chapter of his life would finally be done. It was what he wanted all along; but now that it was staring him in the face, he was scared. Touring and performing were practically all he knew.

His eyes flickered up and backstage. He could just make out the shape of Parker standing at the sidelines and meeting his gaze instantly, as if he sensed Taylor looking for him.

Even with all the lights onstage, and the darkness shrouding Parker, Taylor could clearly make out his beaming smile when their eyes met. The other man shot him a little thumbs-up and mouthed, *You're doing great!*

Taylor managed a watery smile, nodding. One look from Parker was all it took to settle him. Get Well Soon would be over, but nothing would be stopping him from performing in the future. Hell, he owned the damn venue—he could perform every night if he missed it so much. But it would be here, at home, where he wouldn't have to live out of a tour bus and learn a different stage configuration every night. It would be familiar and safe, and he would be here with Parker. *That* was what he wanted. None of the rest of it mattered.

The next song started up, snapping him out of his thoughts; luckily, the intro didn't have any keyboard, so no one noticed how unprepared he suddenly was. If anyone saw the pained expression that must have been on his face, well, surely they would just think it was because of Zach.

Taylor had thought a lot about what he wanted to say when it was his turn to speak, and the words rolled around in his head even as he continued to sing. In the lull between songs, he cleared his throat and leaned closer to his mic. The crowd started cheering before he could even say anything, clearly anticipating what would happen. He laughed, and the crowd cheered louder.

"There's so much I could say and still have more to get through, so I'll try to keep this short," he said.

"No!" someone in the crowd exclaimed, while another shouted, "Tell us!"

He laughed again, shaking his head and trying to gather his thoughts before continuing.

"This was everything to Zach," he finally said. "Being here with the band onstage, touring around to see all of you, wherever you were—this was his dream. This was what he wanted to do for as long as I knew him. I'm really thankful he shared that dream with us, and with you all. I'm thankful for the time I had with him, and with the rest of the band. Kylie, Angie, Dean—" He turned to look back at them. "Thank you for everything, really. I'm so lucky to have friends like you. Thanks for sticking with me through all of this."

Angie grinned widely at him, Kylie blew him a kiss, and Dean only nodded from behind his drum set. Taylor turned back toward the crowd and made a wide gesture.

"Thank you for being here tonight in this new chapter of my life," he continued. "I'm done touring, but I'm so glad to still be sharing music with you all through the Caesura Room. So please keep coming back for more shows. I've never owned a music venue before, but, you know, how hard could it be?"

He laughed, shaking his head. "Thanks to all my new staff, especially Moss, Reid, Jasper, and everyone on the stage crew. Thanks for trusting me, and thanks for making sure this show happened without any issues."

Taylor turned again to look backstage. "And there are some people backstage I need to thank, too. Rogelio, thanks for being a friend of the band during all this. You'll always be welcome here. And Parker…"

He choked up, eyes burning. How could he put into words everything Parker had done for him? How would any thanks possibly ever be enough? Taylor blinked away tears, clearing his throat. He could see Parker's face, his brows furrowed, despite the sweet smile on his face.

"Parker," he repeated. "I couldn't have done this without you. The Caesura Room is as much your baby as it is mine now. You've always been an important part of mine and Zach's story, and part of Get Well Soon's story. I'm so glad to have you in my life still. This one's for you."

If he kept looking at Parker's face, he would really start to cry, so he turned his attention back to the keyboard and smashed his hands down into the opening chords of Wish We Were There.

/ /

I saw you in a dream last night driving next to me
on the highway
Headlights off but the streetlamp followed you all
the way home
It painted you like liquid gold
We were only inches apart
We were only miles apart

Maybe a happy ending isn't in the cards for us
A backyard garden and picket fence somewhere
quiet and suburban
And I know you can see it, too
Don't you wish we were there?

Then you saw me get dragged down in the
undertow
Our friends all watching but only you knew I
couldn't swim
No one else dove in
Our hands were inches apart
We were only miles apart

Maybe a happy ending isn't in the cards for us
A backyard garden and picket fence somewhere
quiet and suburban
And I know you can see it, too
Baby, don't you wish we were there?

How do I get what I want when I don't even know
it?
What more could I want when I already have it?
Did you get what you wanted?
Did you get it?

Maybe a happy ending isn't in the cards for us
A backyard garden and picket fence somewhere
quiet and suburban
And I know you can see it, too
Don't you wish we were there?
Baby, don't you wish we were there?

/ /

Taylor was the last one backstage when the show was over, wiping sweat and tears from his face as he stumbled through the curtain. His heart pounded painfully against his ribs, making him pant for breath. He was finally done. He'd made it through. It was over.

He could barely formulate a thought, only that he wanted Parker. His head swung heavily back and forth, looking, but it was so dark back here compared to the stage, he couldn't make out anything—

"Taylor!" Parker's voice came, and he turned toward it.

"Parker," he replied, and it came out as half a sob. Parker's hands found him, pulling him into a hug, even though he was covered in sweat.

"Hey, you're okay," Parker murmured, holding him tightly. "You're alright. You did it. It's done. It's all done. You did it!"

Taylor's gasps turned into a laugh at the eager, lilting tone Parker took on. "I did it," he croaked.

"You made me cry," Parker murmured, softer now. "You were so amazing out there, Taylor. You were incredible. Zach would be—he would be really proud of you. *I'm* proud of you."

Taylor nodded against his chest, eyes burning. His heart nearly burst with the mess of emotions running through it. Would things ever feel less complicated? Would it ever get any easier? *Would* Zach be proud of him? Why did he still care?

Parker squeezed him closer, lips pressing a soft kiss to his forehead. He'd gotten used to the feel of Parker's beard now, and the soft scratchiness of it against his skin helped ground him. He was here. He was safe. Everything was going to be alright. Maybe he would always have this messy jumble of feelings about how Get Well Soon had ended, but maybe Parker was right. Maybe Zach would be happy for him now.

When he finally managed to pull away and look around, they were the only ones left in the wing. Taylor could hear the faint murmur of a lingering crowd from outside, and the noise of the stage crew working further back. He wiped his eyes, sniffling, then managed a watery smile at Parker.

"I'm okay," he said softly, reading the question in the other man's expression. "I feel a lot... lighter now. I think I'm okay."

Parker nodded, smiling tentatively back at him. "Kylie said they were going to take a few minutes in the green room, then come down to say hello to some of the fans still hanging out. Do you want to do that, too?"

Taylor nodded. "Yeah, that sounds good."

Parker led him back up to the green room, where he chugged an entire bottle of water before even looking for anyone else. The cold water helped snap him back into reality—bringing him down from the floaty, emotional flow state he'd been in—like his vision had been blurred and was suddenly sharpened back into focus.

"You alright, bud?" Kylie asked softly, coming up alongside him. "That was a lot, huh?"

Taylor looped one arm around her shoulders and hugged her. He still felt sweaty, but she made a soft sound and turned entirely into the hug, wrapping both her arms around his chest.

"I told you," she said, her voice muffled against his shoulder. "I told you we were gonna be okay."

He chuckled. "You're right. We'll be okay."

His eyes scanned the room, and he finally caught sight of Rogelio standing in the corner, holding a can of beer close to his chest and looking awkwardly down at it. Dean was slouched against the wall next to him, but Rogelio kept glancing in their direction. Taylor gave Kylie one last squeeze, motioned for Parker to wait for him, then walked over to the two men. Rogelio's eyes landed on him instantly, but Dean didn't glance up to look at him until Taylor was standing right in front of them.

"Hey," Taylor said uncertainly, not quite sure what to say now that he was here. "Sorry I didn't get a chance to say hi to you before the show. But, uh, thanks for coming."

Rogelio pressed his lips together in a semblance of a smile. "Yeah. Thanks for inviting me."

"I meant what I said out there," Taylor replied. "You're always welcome here. I know Zach cared about you, and, well, I guess we all have to take care of each other now, you know? Don't be a stranger."

Rogelio was silent for a moment, looking at him with an unreadable expression. Finally, though, he gave a sharp nod.

"Thanks," he replied simply. He blinked rapidly before looking away. Maybe he was so curt because he was on the verge of tears, though he didn't exactly look it. "I, uh... I appreciate it."

"Told you," Dean said, stifling a grin and glancing over at Rogelio, who rolled his eyes and shoved Dean's shoulder, mumbling something in Spanish.

"I mean it," Taylor repeated. On his way offstage, he'd grabbed the setlist closest to him, and it was folded in his back pocket now. He retrieved it and smoothed it out, gently peeled the blue painter's tape off the edges, then handed it to Rogelio. "Here. You can have this."

Rogelio took it, staring at the paper with quivering hands for a long moment. Zach had given him a setlist from each of the shows he'd tagged along for; Taylor planned on keeping this setlist for himself, but what was the point? He had at least a hundred other Get Well Soon setlists with all his stuff somewhere. Something told him it would mean a lot more to Rogelio than it would mean to him now.

Rogelio cleared his throat as he folded the setlist into careful fourths and slipped it into his jacket pocket. "Thanks, man. I, uh, I appreciate it."

"No problem," Taylor replied. "And you have my number, right? Feel free to reach out if you ever need anything, okay?"

Rogelio nodded, looking away from both him and Dean with glassy eyes. "I will. Thank you."

Chapter Twenty
Parker

Rogelio left in a hurry, but Taylor didn't seem upset—if anything, Parker thought he looked sad to see him go. He watched as Taylor and Dean spoke for a moment longer, then Angie came up alongside them and said something Parker couldn't hear.

Taylor laughed, as did Angie, then Taylor's eyes flickered past them to Parker. Parker's heart sped up—he couldn't stop the smile spreading across his face, but Taylor grinned back and gestured for him to come over.

"I'm going to change my shirt, then we're gonna go down in like ten minutes to say hi to everyone who stayed behind," Taylor said. "Will you come downstairs with me?"

"Change your shirt?" Parker repeated, stifling a laugh. "What do you mean? You look great."

Taylor grimaced. "I get so sweaty after shows. If I'm going to be hugging fans, I'd rather do it in dry clothes."

"Maybe it would be better for me to stay up here if you'll be talking to fans," Parker replied. They had discussed how they didn't want their relationship to be entirely public knowledge yet, at least not until everything with Get Well Soon was officially over.

"But I want you there," Taylor said, sounding shy. "Maybe you can just wait at the bar?"

Parker melted. He didn't think he would ever be able to say no to Taylor for anything. "Sure. I'll wait at the bar."

Ten minutes later, they were shuffling back down the green room stairs, Taylor wearing a clean, fresh shirt.

A group of about twenty people had lingered in hopes of meeting them, some still hanging out near the stage and some at the bar, though they all congregated as Taylor and the band stepped out from side stage and down to greet them. Parker slipped away in all the noise, sitting down at the now-empty bar.

Moss, the new bartender, grinned at him as he sat down. Parker smiled back; he'd only met Moss a few times, but they'd gotten along well when they'd spoken.

"Howdy," they said cheerfully. "On moral support duty, huh?"

Parker laughed, nodding. "Yeah, you could say that." All the staff knew about his and Taylor's relationship, but they also seemed to understand that it wasn't public yet, which was a relief. At least they didn't have to sneak around in the Caesura Room.

"Here," Moss said, setting an opened bottle of beer in front of him. "It's on the house."

Over the next hour, Parker watched as Taylor and the rest of the band hugged and shook the hands of all the fans who had stuck around to see them after the show. Several of them handed Taylor small gifts, or had him sign albums or t-shirts, so many that he had to make a small pile on the stage, a little distance away from all the gifts left at the mic for Zach. Parker worried maybe it would all be too much, too emotionally draining; but every time Taylor looked toward him, he shot Parker a small smile.

Eventually, though, all the lingering fans eventually shuffled out into the night, leaving the band alone in front of the stage. Parker had done his best to chat with Moss, and not eavesdrop too much, but now the venue was much quieter with only a handful of people left. He propped his head up in one hand, elbow on the bar, and watched as the four band members seemed to look silently at each other, as if trying to judge what to do next.

Finally, it was Taylor who offered, "Well... I guess that's it."

Dean snorted, rolling his eyes. Angie smacked his shoulder again, but was stifling a laugh herself.

"Ladies, gentlemen, it's been an honor," Kylie said with an exaggerated bow, which only made Angie giggle more. "Taylor, I have to hand it to you. Being able to drive myself home after a show is definitely better than getting on a tour bus."

Taylor laughed. "I think so, too."

Parker chuckled, and Taylor's head shot in his direction, looking flustered to realize that he was watching. Kylie laughed, waving at him; Parker only raised his beer bottle to them. He would give them their space—it seemed important that they have their last moments as a band together without an intruder.

They talked amongst themselves quietly for a little longer, but Parker could only focus on Taylor. He'd been so nervous about the show for the past week, and his relief was all but palpable—in the way he was holding himself, how easily he smiled, and the sweet lilt of his voice. Even now, in the unglamorous light, Parker swore he almost seemed to glow.

Eventually, though, the group seemed to wrap up whatever they were discussing. Angie and Dean stepped away, the first to leave, waving goodbye as they headed for the exit.

Taylor and Kylie exchanged something in hushed tones for a little longer, then they looked over at him, both smiling.

"Bye, Parker!" Kylie exclaimed with an exaggerated wave. Parker returned the wave with a confused smile. He had no idea what they were saying about him, but Taylor had a small, fond smile on his face, so it must have been good.

"Bye," he replied uncertainly, but she was already turning to go.

Taylor joined him at the bar. Moss had been idly wiping down the counter, but when he sat down, they pulled a bottle of the same beer Parker was drinking from the fridge and set it in front of Taylor, who laughed and took it.

"Thanks, Moss," he said, and they shot him a wink.

"Figured you'd want something to wind down with," they said. "I've got some dishes to do in the back, so give me a shout if you need anything. Or, you know, take whatever you want. It's your bar."

"Will do," Taylor laughed. The door to the back-of-house swung shut behind them, then it was only Parker and Taylor left. Even though he knew Moss was in the back, and Reid and the stage crew were probably still around, for now, they were alone—like it was just the two of them again, fixing up the old, outdated venue all those months ago.

In that moment, they might have been the only ones in the world, sitting with their thighs pressed together at the bar. Maybe the timing wasn't good, but he was sure he couldn't keep the words down any longer.

Even watching from the sidelines, Taylor had been so incredible to witness. He had been like an angel on the stage: the moody lighting cast long shadows from his eyelashes down his face, alternating between a dreamy half-lidded expression when he would look down at his keyboard, and illuminating his eyes into a bright, pearlescent blue when he looked up and out toward the audience, or toward Parker.

He had known it maybe since the beginning, but the words couldn't be held back any longer. He *had* to say something.

"That was really nice of you," he said softly, looking down at his beer on the bar in front of him. "Back when you were onstage... It was really sweet of you to say that. I hope you know I was happy to help with everything."

Taylor's gaze softened as he smiled. "I know. But I really meant it, Parker. I want... Well, I hope you'd want to be part of the Caesura Room forever."

Parker's heart stuttered, all but bursting out of his chest. How had he ever gotten so lucky that someone as incredible as Taylor wanted to be with *him*? His mouth worked silently for a moment, trying to say something just as sweet, something just as heartfelt; but his mind kept going back to the same three-word phrase.

He had never been unsure of his feelings, but that same familiar worry of moving too fast had kept him from saying it. Now, though, it seemed like the only thing left he could say after witnessing something so sublime.

"I love you," Parker said, the words all leaving him in a rush, like he'd unplugged a dam. "You were so incredible up on the stage, Taylor, you're just... You're the most important person in the world to me. I love you, and I want to be part of your life for as long as you'll have me."

Taylor had frozen beside him, eyes wide and shining as a faint pinkish flush rose in his cheeks. But then a slow smile spread across his face, and warmth flooded Parker's heart.

"I love you, too," Taylor said, reaching over to grab both his hands. He let out a nervous laugh, but his smile was pure and genuine. "Fuck, I was amping myself up to say it first."

Parker laughed, squeezing his hands. "I guess we both were."

"I love you, Parker," Taylor repeated, the words coming out breathlessly, like he couldn't wait to say them. "I love you. I *love* you."

Parker leaned closer and kissed him. Taylor made a soft, muffled noise against his mouth, kissing him back fervently. He had been just as sure of Taylor's feelings as he had been of his own; but hearing Taylor say it, repeating it like he'd wanted to say it a hundred times before—how could he do anything but kiss him? The tension that had been building in his body drained away all at once, filling him with a bright, euphoric relief in its place.

Taylor loved him. Taylor wanted to be with him. Taylor wanted him around forever. It was everything Parker had ever dreamed of.

Taylor's warm hands were cupping his face, holding him close, even as he broke their kiss to say it again. "I love you, too, Taylor," he murmured, the other man's lips brushing against his own as he spoke. He felt Taylor smile.

"You know, maybe I *will* still play piano," he said softly. "If it gets this kind of reaction out of you..."

Parker chuckled before pressing another kiss to his lips. "I'll be your most dedicated fan. I'll make it to every show."

Taylor's expression melted from one of amusement to something much more sincere. "I forgot how much I like performing, to be honest. Touring and all that sucked, but being onstage... That's the good part, you know? And if you like it, too, maybe I will."

Parker could tell his expression must have been sappy and adoring, but he couldn't help it—even remembering how beautiful Taylor had been in the stage lights was enough to make his heart skip a beat. "Whatever you want to do, but honestly, I would love that."

Before Taylor could respond, Moss came through the back-of-house door, carrying a bucket of clean glasses. They didn't say anything, but Parker could tell from their stifled grin that they had probably seen the scene play out between him and Taylor through the window in the door, waiting until they'd had their moment to return to the bar.

Taylor must have noticed the same thing; he hid a laugh behind his hand and swiveled in his bar seat to face back out toward the stage, his back pressed against the bar countertop. Parker turned to look: the stage crew had started breaking down the equipment, packing instruments away, and pulling up cords from where they'd been taped down. The venue had come back to life around them. Still, this little piece of it was Taylor's—theirs.

"You know," he said softly, interlacing his fingers with Taylor's. "I think this is shaping up to become something really amazing."

Taylor's eyes were full of hope as he smiled in response. "I think so, too."

Epilogue
Taylor
Six Months Later

"You're not going to fucking believe who I just fucking booked."

Taylor and Parker looked up, surprised, from where they'd been sitting on the balcony. Parker's laptop was open in front of him as he worked on an article; Taylor had come up here to work alongside him, humming softly to himself while scrolling through an email on his phone. They had heard footsteps coming up the balcony stairs, but the appearance of Sadie—the Caesura Room's booking agent—was a surprise. She was panting as she stood at the top of the stairs, as if she'd come running from her office to find them.

"Who?" Taylor asked, frowning as he started to stand up—but then Sadie laughed, running an incredulous hand through her long, purple hair. Her circular glasses made her eyes look huge with excitement. "I just got off the phone with Jason Daugherty's manager," she burst out. "They're going on tour with the Astral Complex." Taylor blinked, the words processing for a moment, but Parker's mouth dropped open instantly.

For the past several months the Caesura Room had been open, the final show for Get Well Soon had been the biggest show they'd put on. Since then, they'd had many open mic nights, and several smaller, more local queer-fronted groups had put on shows as well, but nothing huge. Nothing like this.

"Holy shit," Parker said, laughing in shock. "Seriously? Together?"

Sadie nodded, and it all hit Taylor in a rush. Synesthesia was putting out a new album, but it was also the ten-year anniversary of *Dying to Leave,* the breakup album that had defined their careers—there was no way that wasn't intentional, even if the tour wasn't for that album specifically.

"Didn't you interview Jason last year?" Taylor asked, looking back at Parker, who nodded. "Did you know he was going to do this?"

"No, when I talked to him, he had a new album in the works, but this..." Parker started, then shook his head. "I'm seriously shocked. I tried to talk to him about Sterling and the Astral Complex a bit, but his agent pulled the plug as soon as he was mentioned, so... I don't know. It seemed like maybe Jason wanted to make amends, but I have no idea how he might have managed to convince Sterling to do something like *this*."

"I *know!*" Sadie squealed with delight. "This is going to be huge. And they're playing here! *Here!*"

Parker laughed, glancing sidelong at Taylor. "He asked me about you when I interviewed him, now that I think about it."

Taylor stared at them both a moment longer, still absorbing the situation. Even though Synesthesia was surely no longer in their heyday, and The Astral Complex had never been as commercially successful as Jason's band, the fact that they would be touring together for the anniversary of their own breakup album was... He couldn't decide if it was painfully tacky, or some genius marketing move. Maybe a little bit of both.

"Wow," he finally said simply, unsure of what else to say. "That's... Yeah, that's wild. I bet that whole tour is gonna be sold out. They knew what they were doing for sure."

"I wonder how they convinced Sterling to come out of retirement," Sadie murmured, the question sounding as innocuous as if she were talking about her own relative, and not a public figure that hadn't been heard from in half a decade. Then she gasped, eyes growing even wider. "Oh my god, you guys, what if they *got back together*? Is that why they're doing this?!"

Taylor laughed; considering how cruel a picture *Dying to Leave* had painted, that seemed incredibly unlikely. "I really, really doubt that, Sadie."

"We could start up a betting pool," Parker suggested, and Sadie howled with laughter.

"Well, keep me posted if you do," she said, shooting Taylor a grin before turning back toward the stairs. "I'll get back to work, boss. I just had to rant about this to someone. I still can't believe it."

She was hurrying back down the stairs before either could respond, her boots thudding heavily on the metal steps. Taylor looked back over at Parker; the other man had an incredulous expression still. "I can't wait to tell Kylie about this," Taylor laughed, and Parker shook his head.

"How much do you want to bet the tour gets canceled before it even starts?" he murmured, and Taylor laughed aloud.

"Oh, god. You know, I wouldn't be surprised if it *does* get canceled... But I hope it happens," he replied. "Maybe it means they've put things behind them and can maybe get along now. But mostly, if it does happen, I'm sure we're gonna have a full house."

Parker blinked, the realization only just seeming to dawn on him—Taylor fought back a grin at his adorably surprised expression. "Wow, yeah. This'll be the biggest act to ever book the Caesura Room so far, huh? I mean, not including Get Well Soon."

Taylor chuckled and waved his hand dismissively. "That didn't count. Plus, it wasn't *booked.*"

Parker laughed, but worry had already started to bubble up in Taylor's chest. He bit his lip and peered over the railing, eyes sweeping over the small stage, the pit, the meager seating by the bar and balcony...

"Shit, will we even have room for a show that size?" he wondered, looking back at Parker with his brows furrowed. But Parker only smiled in return, reaching over to squeeze his hand reassuringly.

"That's a good problem to have, isn't it?" he replied, and Taylor couldn't disagree. "It's way too early to worry about that now, Taylor. If it's a sold out show, then it's a sold out show. And if we need to rearrange some things to try to fit a few more customers in the back... well, we'll figure it out. We'll make it work."

That was all true. They only had so much space, and a sold-out show would be hectic, but hopefully in a good way.

"I love you," Taylor said, smiling back at Parker. "You always know what to say to make me feel better."

Parker grinned. He was trying to look suave about it, but Taylor could see the pleased flush rising in his cheeks, the way his eyes crinkled with affection when he smiled. It made his own chest fill with butterflies.

"Hey, that's what I'm here for," Parker replied, then added more softly, "And I love you, too, baby."

He leaned a little closer, and Taylor met him halfway. He could feel Parker's smile against his lips.

When they pulled away, all he could think about was how glad he was that they were alone up here, so no one else could see the sappy, blissed-out expression that must have been on his face as he held Parker's gaze. He was so incredibly lucky to have had a second chance with Parker; every day, the impossibility of it all struck him anew. But here they were: this was their life together, against all odds.

"God, don't look at me like that when we're at work," Parker whispered, and Taylor laughed, finally pulling away.

"What, you don't like looking at me?" he fake-pouted, settling back into his seat beside Parker. Their shoulders brushed up against each other, then Parker put his arm around Taylor's waist, tugging him a little closer.

"You know that's not true," Parker murmured, pressing another kiss to the side of his neck, this one full of heat.

But then he pulled away all at once, his hands reaching for the laptop on the table in front of them again, a bemused expression falling over his face. "But I *really* need to finish this article today, baby."

"I guess I should get back to work, too," Taylor sighed, but he still had the same sappy smile on his face.

His thoughts lingered on what Parker had said as they each returned to their tasks.

He was right—they would figure it out. They would make it work, just like they always had.

THE END

Thank you for reading Wish We Were There! For a sweet and steamy bonus epilogue, please sign up for my email newsletter here or at my website, lionelhart.ink

If you enjoyed this book, please consider leaving a rating or review. It truly helps more than you know! This book has been my first foray into contemporary MM romance, so your feedback is highly appreciated. Thank you!

As you might have guessed, book two of The Caesura Room is going to be a second chance romance between Jason, the struggling rockstar Parker interviewed, and the mysterious Sterling Sloane. Keep an eye out for a preorder link coming soon.

Lionel Hart (he/him) is an indie author of MM fantasy romance and paranormal romance. Currently, he resides in north San Diego with his husband and their dog. For personal updates and new releases, follow the links below.

Website: lionelhart.ink

YouTube: @LionelHartAuthor

Twitter: @lionelhart_

Facebook: Lionel Hart, Author

TikTok: @author.lionelhart

Email Newsletter

You can find all my books at books.lionelhart.ink

Fantasy

<u>Chronicles of the Veil</u>

1. The Changeling Prophecy

2. The Drawn Arrow

3. The Blighted Sky

4. The Sacrificial Heart

<u>Heart of Dragons Duology</u>

1. Beneath His Wings

2. By Fang and Fire

<u>The Orc Prince Trilogy</u>

1. Claimed by the Orc Prince

2. Blood of the Orc Prince

3. Ascension of the Orc King

Contemporary

The Caesura Room

1. Wish We Were There

2. Dying to Leave – coming 2024

Printed in Great Britain
by Amazon

44005276R00169